Curse
Of the
Quill

Curse of the Quill

Library of Congress 10 9 8 7 6 5 4 3 2 1

Curse
Of the
Quill

A Quill Lost in Time Book 2

J.L. Hinds

More works by J.L. Hinds.

Check them out at www.authorjlhinds.com
and by following the author on TikTok,
Instagram, Threads, and Facebook.

Thank you, my loving husband Tim.
You've been so supportive
throughout my whole writing career. I
truly appreciate everything you've
done for me and what you continue to
do. Lusvvvm.

To all my family and friends, thank
you from the bottom of my heart. I
love you all.

I wasn't always this way. Before my 18th birthday, I was just a normal kid who did normal things, well most of the time. I had a best friend, although I wished she would've been more.

Listen, I don't claim to be a saint in the slightest, I have my faults. Before you go judging me on what I did, hear me out. I'm going to take it back to the beginning when everything started. Maybe that will give you a little insight into me and what I had to go through.

I *did* truly care for Adilyne Grace. I think I had fallen for her. That's what made all this so hard, but I just had to get that quill and journal away from her. I knew if I didn't, it would have destroyed her.

Here's *my* story…

Earlier in the day a strange man approached her. At first, she thought he was just a panhandler trying to hit her up for money, but she soon found out she was *sorely* mistaken. What happened in the moments following, she could never forget

3

until her last breath.

"What do you want from us?" She asked the strange man, rolling the stroller around that held her precious baby boy. She wanted to put as much distance as she could between the man and Tallon. She didn't know what he wanted but she would be damned if he got anywhere near her baby.

He looks towards Tallon then back at her. She steps further away from the man, making sure to widen the distance.

"NO! You are not having my baby!" She couldn't believe the gall of this man to indicate wanting her child. There is not a chance in the universe that she would give

4

him up. Not even if she was given a million

dollars or more. She loved and cherished

him more than anything.

She could feel the anger bubbling to the

surface. She needed to put as much space as

she could between this man and Tallon.

"I'm not here to take your baby." He said

as he reached in his pocket and revealed a

quill and notebook. The quill was

enchantingly beautiful. The feather was a

purple hue fading into black. The pen of the

quill was a stunning silver with a fleur-de-lis

design carved through it.

The notebook was an ancient brown

leather- bound book with a strap as the

enclosure. He unwrapped the strap from the notebook and wrote something in it. After he was done, he closed the notebook then out the corner of her eye something was happening.

She turned her head to find Tallon glowing, a bright purple haze surrounded his little body. Her eyes widen as she picks him up, the glow fading.

"What have you done to him..." She said as she held him in her arms, rocking side to side. When she looked up, the man was gone.

"What in the world?!" She looked all around; he was nowhere to be found. It was as though he had just vanished out of nowhere. She looks over Tallon, checking every inch of his little body.

"What did he do to you, my sweet boy? Let's go home, I believe that was enough excitement for you to last a lifetime." She kissed his forehead and placed him back in the stroller. She was relieved to find nothing wrong with him. At least, not on the outside. There was no telling what damage was caused internally.

Once she arrived home, she put up the stroller, carried Tallon on her hip and put him in his crib. She noticed his eyes

drooping, indicating he was sleepy.

Well, of course he would be tired,

they had a long frightening day. She

wouldn't be surprised if he actually slept

through the entire night. She sat back in the

rocking chair, keeping her eyes glued to

Tallon. His little chest raising and falling as

he slept. She envied how he sleeps. If only

she could. There's no way she'll be able to

do much now. She still had that strange

man's image in her head. She still couldn't

understand what had happened. It was too

much of a coincidence. Whatever he wrote

with that quill in that journal, had *something*

to do with Tallon, she just couldn't figure it out.

She sat back on the chair, leaning her head back and staring up at the ceiling. She felt wide awake, there was no way she would be able to sleep now. She knew she had to keep an eye on her baby, she wanted to make sure he was okay.

Gina jumped and almost fell out of the rocking chair she hadn't realized she had fallen asleep. She looked up to find Tallon sitting up in his crib staring at her with tears falling down his cheeks.

"What's wrong my sweet boy?" she asked as she got up to reach for him. She could tell by the sound of his cry it could only mean one thing... A bad dream. She rocked him side to side in her arms. "Shhh… mommies got you. Nothing's gonna happen to you I'm right here to protect you always and forever." He started to calm down, then closed his eyes drifting back to sleep.

Two weeks later

Gina was relieved to find nothing was wrong with her baby. Every day she sat there watching him worried, but he just played like any other normal baby happy and carefree. Although everything seemed okay, she couldn't relax too much. She just knew something was going to happen, he just didn't know when she knew she had to keep her guard up.

Last week she had taken him to the doctor just to be on the safe side to make sure that he was okay. The doctor said he was perfectly healthy he saw nothing wrong with any tests that he ran. She was relieved to hear that all the tests came back normal, she felt some comfort in that, but something still bothered her.

As the days turned into weeks, in the

weeks turned into years her guard started to

drop more and more. She started to come to

terms that maybe it was all in her head.

Chapter One

Eighteen Years Later...

As I walk into the living room, I turn and see my mother through the pass through between the living room and kitchen. The shades folded out on each side. I walk and sit at one of the stools, resting my elbows on the counter.

"Today's finally the day!" I'm finally a legal adult. "I know dear. I *am* your mother after all." She replies with a smirk. Of course, she would say something like that.

"Yep, I'm 18. You know what that means, right?" I tease her, knowing full well it'll drive her crazy. A weird look appears on her face for a split

second before she plasters on a smile and looks up from the bowl. "You alright?" I ask. Lately she's been a little antsy and seems to be a little on edge. She doesn't think I see it, but I've noticed a lot more recently.

"I'm fine, dear. What makes you

think something's wrong?" She puts the bowl down and takes the skillet off the burner and places it on a hot pad by the stove.

"Nothing." I say shaking my head. She walks over to me and wraps my hands in hers. "So… Have any plans for your birthday? A day out with friends?" She says with a wink. I can't help but laugh. I don't think she even tries to be funny, but I love it.

I think of what I'm going to do today. I guess I could start looking for my own place. God knows I'm not going to live with my mom my entire life. I'm an adult now

15

and I need to act the part.

I started by getting a part-time job working nights and weekends and I managed to save enough money for a down payment and a couple months' rent. That should keep me going until I can find a full-time job after graduation.

"Yeah, I guess I could hang out with the guys tonight. Graduation is just a week away so tonight could be a twofer. Graduation and Birthday celebration." The more I think about it the more pumped I get. Tonight, ought to be fun.

16

It's 5:30 pm and I put the finishing touches on my outfit. Deciding to keep it semi casual, I chose a pair of faded blue jeans, a black tee shirt and a sports coat.

I glance at my reflection one last time, grabbing each opening of my coat. "That'll do" I say to myself as I head out the door.

The boys were all too pumped to go out. They wanted any excuse to get away from their families for the evening. We decided on The O Club Bar & Grill.

Not only do they have a bar and dining, but they also have a dance floor, darts games, and my favorite thing about it is the two rows of pool tables.

My friends and I would always look through the big bay window in the front and watch as people played pool, wishing we could go in. At The O Club you had to be eighteen or older to go in and since we were only sixteen at the time, we weren't allowed. They were

afraid we would get ahold of alcohol just when an inspector or officer was in, and they would lose their

license.

"It's about time dude." Jacob says as he slaps

my back. He and Elijah turned ei a few

months ago and waited on me so we could

go together. "I know right.

Let's go." I say as we head inside, making

our way straight for the pool tables.

We spent two hours playing pool. After

beating both their asses, they both kept

hounding for 'best two out of three' and so

on. I just kept laughing and bringing it on. I

never grow tired of seeing the smug looks

on their faces fade into looks of

disappointment every time I beat them.

I set my sights on the last ball, the eight ball, lining it up for a perfect corner shot. I reared my cue back and took my shot. We watch as the white ball hits the eight ball. Then the eight ball goes right into the corner pocket. "… And that's how you do it boys." I say as I throw my cue down onto the table.

They wave their arms at me, shooing me away. "Lucky shot birthday boy." Eli says as we make our way to the dining table. "It's just my lucky night." I smirk as we take a seat. We order our food and Jacob gets up to go to the bathroom.

"So… Where are you heading off to after graduation? I think I'm gonna take a year off and travel some. My parents don't like the idea of me spending the money they saved for college being 'blown' on traveling, but they can't tell me what to do now that I'm an adult. I just assured them I would save any extra money and go to college when I've seen all there is to see. Eventually they saw reason." Eli explains. "That's a good question." I answer. What *am* I going to do after graduation? I never really thought about it. I've just been working extra hard these past two years, making sure I make it to graduation. "What? You don't know? Dude, graduation's next week. You need to figure *something* out." I squint my eyes at him and tilt my head.

21

"Why do I *have* to figure it out before graduation? My mom isn't kicking me out yet. I still have some time. I may just move out to the beach and relax some, save money and get a good job." I reply.

My mom's had it hard with me. I haven't made it easy for her. From the stories she's told me, my 'father', if you could call him that, left her at the hospital after I was born. Apparently, he told her he wasn't 'ready' to be a father yet. I don't think she needed him anyway. She did a pretty good job on her own. I'm still here, aren't I?

"Yo… Earth to Tallon. Did you hear a word I said?" Jacob says waving a hand in front of my face. I

blink rapidly and look at him. When did he

get back? "Sorry, I guess I was just lost in

thought." "I'd say so. You looked like you

were a million miles away. You had me

worried." He laughed. I did too. I didn't

think you could be so lost in thought you

don't realize what's going on around you.

Our food arrives and they start

digging in, like they haven't eaten in weeks.

I laugh at them. I put my hand above the

table, reaching for the fork. Suddenly, a

sharp pain slices through my upper arm. I

grab it and groan.

"What's wrong, Tallon?" Eli says as

he starts to get up out of his chair. I stopped him. "Don't worry about it. It may just be a cramp. It'll go away in a sec." I told him. I don't need anyone smothering me.

I get up and walk to the bathroom. Once I shut the door behind me, I lock it. When I grabbed my arm at the table, I felt something odd under my shirt. I lift up my sleeve and see shimmering scales where my skin is supposed to be. WHAT THE HELL?! The pain is simmered, and a weird sensation takes its place. I look at the scales on my arm and they are blue in color, with some specs of magenta, yellow, and green in them.

Chapter Two

This has *got* to be some sort of nightmare or something. How can I have scales on my arm?! I pull my sleeve back down and walk back to the table as though nothing is wrong.

"What's up? Are you okay, man? You were in there a good while. You need a

Pepto or something?" Jake says and we all laugh. He really knows how to lighten a mood. I punched him on the shoulder. "No, I don't need '*Pepto*'. There was a line, I had to wait." I lie. They don't need to know I may be growing scales. They'd definitely think I'd gone insane.

"I think I'm gonna call it a night. Today's been fun, but I'm beat." The pain in my arm's starting to come back and now I'm starting to feel some tiny needle pricks in my other arm. I need to get out of here.

Rubbing my tingling arm, low and behold it feels like scales, the same as my other arm. I have *got* to ask mom what's

26

going on. This can't be normal.

"Already? It's still early." Eli says as he looks at his watch. "It's only 8:45. Are you sure you're, okay?" I can tell he's concerned and I'm sure it's nothing but in case I'm wrong, I don't want to chance it.

"Yeah E, I'm good. I'll see you guys tomorrow, okay?" I say as I turn to head out. They wish me a happy birthday as I go.

I walk through the front door and notice my mom sitting on the recliner, a book resting on her chest. She's passed out.

27

She must've been waiting for me to get home.

I take the bookmark that's resting on the side table next to her and place it in the place she stopped. I put the book on the table and covered her with the lap blanket. I kiss her forehead and head to bed.

I reached for my door and a sharp pain hit my gut. I lift my shirt and find scales. The same scales that had appeared on my arm. What in the hell is happening to me? I lift my sleeves and the scales seem to be spreading. Suddenly, I feel what could only be described as growing pains. My skull feels like it's doubling in size. I ran to the back door and out to the yard, holding my aching head. As I got to the middle of the yard, I doubled over, and my knees hit the ground.

"What the…" I look down at my hands and all of a sudden, they start to change. Claws take the place of my fingers. Scales replace my skin, and my arms start to grow three times their size, membranes and scaly bones take shape.

I scream as my limbs start to grow. Scales appear all over my body. As I transform, my clothes rip off and fall to the ground.

After about thirty grueling minutes of shooting stinging pain of scales growing, screaming as wings shoot out where my arms once were, a tail grows and when it finally stops, I stand roughly ten feet tall.

I look down at what are supposed to be my feet. In their place are two ginormous scale-covered paws. I lift my hands to my face. "Ahh." I try to shout as I look at two claws where my hands used to be.

I look down and around at my body, holy shit! I don't look human at all. Lifting my head up, I glance at the star covered sky. *Can I breathe fire too?* I take a deep breath and blow out. Sure, enough a big stream of

30

flames shot out of my mouth. It didn't even hurt either.

I try to take one step forward and trip over my own feet... well paws. I fall face first into the dirt, missing the ten-foot fence by a hair. The ground shakes, almost like a mini earthquake.

"Son of a snitch!" I try and shout, but it comes out rougher and gruffy. I push myself up with my "arms" and stand on all fours. I look at one side then another. What used to be my arms and hands, are now ginormous wings and claws. As I tried to stand, I toppled over. Looking back, I realize a have a huge, spiked tail on my backside. I need to be slower this time. I slowly and methodically push myself back up to standing. *Success!*

I wonder if I can fly. I look at my ginormous wings and try to flap them like a bird. Nothing happens, just a bunch of wind, knocking over the patio furniture on the back porch. Maybe this is going to be harder than I thought.

I go to try again… "Ahhhh…" I hear as my mom stands on the back porch. Her eyes start drooping and she starts to go limp, her eyes closing. She's fainting. I try and move swiftly and carefully to catch her before her head hits the concrete. Luckily, she lands in

a membrane portion of my wing. I move
slowly to lay her on the grass.

I lay next to her. "Mom! Mom!" I say
in my gruffy voice. I hope she can
understand me. I'm scared and I need her to
be okay. I don't know what I would do
without her. She slowly blinks, her eyes
open. Then they grow wide when they land
on me. She lifts her upper body up and
scoots hurriedly away from me.
"Wh…wh… What do you want? Wwwhere
did you
come from?" She asks me visibly shaking. I
hate seeing her like this. "It's me, mom. It's
Tallon." I try to talk a little slower, hoping

33

she understands me.

Her eyes grow wide and tears pool threatening to fall. As she looks me in the eyes. She seems to recognize me a little. "TTTallon? How? Why?..." She wrings her hands and stares into my eyes. Her gaze turns soft, and tears fall down her cheeks.

She holds out her hands and reaches for my snout. She gently rubs, in a way a mother does when she holds her baby. "Oh, my sweet boy. What happened to you?" After looking me all over, she gasps and covers her mouth with both hands, as though she's realizing something. "No no no… It can't be." She says barely above a whisper.

"What is it? Do you know what's happening to me?" I question. She places her face in her hands and shakes her head, sobbing harder now. I slowly bring my face towards her. Being careful not to knock her down.

She looks at me, tears still falling. "I think I know a little of what's going on. The only thing it could possibly be that could explain this whole mess." Although I want her to hurry and get to the point, I don't push her. This whole thing is hard on not just me, but her as well.

"When you were a baby, I took you to the market. While we were there, a strange man approached us and he had this quill and notebook…" Okay, where's she going with this? I'm not liking it so far. A *strange* man? Why didn't she just turn and walk the other way? "… He wrote something in the journal and your body started to glow a purple aura around you. It was there for only a second, then it was gone. I just thought I was going crazy and had imagined it. Nothing happened to you and when I took you home, I checked you all over and watched you carefully. You seemed perfectly normal…" *Normal*! This doesn't look *normal*. This is as far from normal as a person could get.

"I have no clue what he had written,

but I am positive it had something to do with what's happening to you." She continued.

Hold on a damn minute. Is she saying what I think she's saying?

"Are you trying to tell me that I was *cursed*?!" I cannot believe this! Why me?! How does this happen in real life? I thought it was something people made up in stories and movies. Looking at the sky above me, I close my eyes and do my best to breathe away the anxiety building to the surface.

After a moment I look back down at my mother. Her face falls and I can see the concern and guilt emanating from her. I know I shouldn't be mad at her. I don't want her to think it was her fault. *Somebody* wanted this to happen to me and they would've probably gotten to me one way or another. Now I just need to figure out who it is and reverse what's been done.

Chapter Three

After what happened the other night, I don't know what's going to happen. Will it last for the rest of my life, or just until I find the person responsible?

All I could get out of my mom is a symbol she noticed on the journal and the quill. I need to do some research on that fleur de lis and figure out what the hell is going on.

"Hey T, what happened last night? You left in such a rush. I tried to call you later that night after you left, but you never answered. You feel better?" Eli said as I walked down the hallway. How could I tell him? I don't need him to think I'm crazy and making up stories.

"I'm feeling much better. It must've been something I ate or something. After I got home, I was out of it. I guess I just slept so hard, I didn't hear my phone." Yeah, that sounds convincing enough. It seemed to convince him because he nodded his head.

"That's good man. I'm glad you're okay. Look, it's only three days until graduation. I hope you are still good by then. See ya later man." He slaps my back then heads down the hall.

To be honest, I'm as far from good as I can get. Every night since that night has been the same. Although it's getting easier for me since I've figured out the timing. The clearing in the woods a few miles from my house has been the best place to go when the time comes to change.

It hasn't been easy looking for the mysterious guy who cursed me as a dragon. It's still a foreign concept to me, *dragon*.

Although I turn every single damn night, I
still can't wrap my brain around the fact that
I'm a man by day and a mythical dragon by
night. The worse part of it is, when I change
back into myself, I am left with these
irritating scales along my chest and arms.
My life has been turned upside down
because of this curse. Any normal man my
age would be excited and enthusiastic to
have the ability to turn into a dragon. Me,
however, knowing what happens and what I
have to go through, adds in the fact that I
have to deal with the anxiety of dealing with
scales and finding the person responsible,
make it a curse.

After school, I drive home. There's so much I need to do before the dreaded turn. I've had to change my wardrobe to include all long-sleeved shirts to hide the scales marring my arms.

As soon as I get home, I go straight to my laptop. I need to track down the man responsible for this curse and ask him why me. Why did he do this to me and make him fix what he did, even if I have to get violent.

I power up the computer and type in "Fleur-de- lis Quill and Notebook" Into the search bar. All that pops up is info about different quill pen articles and notebook articles in Paris. I scrolled down and find an interesting article about a castle. I click on the link and wait for it to load.

> *Searles is the oldest castle in New Hampshire.*

Built in 1905, Searles Castle has been the most mysterious architecture in the entire country.

> *After the mysterious disappearance of the owner, Edward Searles, and his wife, Searles Castle has remained abandoned.*

No one knows to this day where the Searles

couple disappeared too. All that was left

was a quill and notebook with the Fleur-

De-Lis design engraved on them...

Wow, that's crazy! This sounds like it might be the place. I type in "Searles Castle" in the search bar and write down the address.

Hopefully I can finally get some answers and get to the bottom of why I was the one who he had to choose. I shut down my computer and get my phone out. How far is the castle from here? I hope it's close enough. Even if it's not, I'm going no matter what. I just need to come up with a plan before making the trip.

Maybe I could just go in the middle of the night when everyone's asleep and fly in my dragon form. That would definitely be cheaper and faster.

I stare at the ceiling, my eyes feeling heavier, suddenly a sharp pain shoots up my arm and I grab it as I sit up quickly.

Glancing at my watch, I realize it's that stupid time of night… 9:00pm. Time for the unfortunate event to happen again.With the pain coursing throughout my body, I quickly make my way to the back yard. Thankfully we live in BFE so there's no chance any neighbors would be able to see what happens.

After my feet hit the grass, I start shedding my clothes. I'm not going to ruin any more of my wardrobe. This curse is starting to cost me financially just in clothing, I swear.

"Darling, why didn't you go to the cave? I thought you were going to make your change there to prevent anyone from seeing you. You know people tend to drive down that road every so often," my mom says as she walks out. I try my best to explain that I wasn't paying attention to the time, but she doesn't seem to hear what I'm saying.

47

"I don't want to hear your excuses. The last thing we need right now is someone to find out about you and cause a panic. If people realize you're a dragon, the authorities will take you away and do God knows what with you. Hurry and get to the cave before someone sees you," she urges as she places her hand on my giant claw.

Although I'm a huge dragon that towers over the house and spits fire, she still sees her boy. I am so relieved Mom doesn't view me as the monster I see. It would hurt me to see the fear in her eyes, but it's not there. I nod my head and start in the direction of the cave. After my first change,

I had to find somewhere remote and away from civilization to endure this. We didn't want any chance of someone spotting me and word gets out that I'm a monster.

When I get to the cave, I duck my giant head just enough to allow room for me to get in. After reaching the end, I take a turn, kind of like a dog, and get into a comfortable position and lay down. It's the only thing that seems to pass the time until I turn back to my normal self.

As I drift to sleep, something in the

49

front of the cave startles me. *What the hell?!*
No one's supposed to be here.

I quickly and quietly get up and shuffle
to the far back corner, away from any light
shining through the cave. It sounds like
someone trying to walk as quietly as they
can, but with my big ole dragon ears, I hear
everything. Leaning my head to the side, I
look as best I can. An old man with a lantern
walks forward, looking all around like he's
trying to find something in particular.

He takes a deep breath and squints his
eyes towards the back of the cave. He starts
forward slowly, getting even closer to where
I am. I try my best to camouflage myself to

the wall of the cave. I hold my breath and narrow my eyes, hoping it's dark enough that he won't see me.

As he nears closer to me, a sound comes from his pocket, and he takes out some kind of object. The object glows a purple hue and has a faint symbol on it. I squint my eyes a little to get a closer look, and I cannot believe my eyes. It's the same symbol that my mom described was on the quill I was cursed with.

The glow dies down, and I do my best to hold back the gasp that wants to escape.

It's *the* QUILL…

Chapter Four

I can't believe it! The stranger I have been searching for this whole time, the one who caused this curse eighteen years ago, is standing right in front of me.

The old man turns and heads towards the entrance of the cave. I guess he didn't find who he was looking for. As he heads further away, I follow him as quietly as I can. I need to know where he goes so, I can track him down later.

I follow behind him through the woods. Every time the stranger turns to look behind him, I hide behind one of the giant redwood trees we pass. Luckily, they are large enough to hide my enormous dragon form, and he has yet to spot me.

After roughly thirty tiring minutes of walking, we come to a castle. *Wait a minute! This castle looks familiar.*

I stop and take a closer look at the property. I watch from the edge of the woods behind the trees as he walks into the castle.

53

So, this is where you live! I finally found you!

Slowly walking around the grounds, being careful to stay out of sight, I take in the scenery. Once I get to the back, it clicks. This is *the* castle. The one that I have looked up and planned on visiting later. I was right. I have got to tell Mom and see this man. There must to be a way for him to reverse this curse he put on me as a baby.

"Mom!" I shout as I walk through the door. I'm so glad I'm back to my normal human self.

"Yes dear. What is it?" she answers as

she walks into the living room. She takes one look at me and rushes towards me. I must look shocked or confused because she can tell something's up.

"What's wrong, Tallon? You look perplexed," she asks worriedly.

"You won't believe what happened at the cave today. While I was there, someone came in." It all comes out in one breath. Before I can continue, she holds up her hand to stop me, looking frustrated.

"WHAT?! Someone saw you! I can't believe it. That was supposed to be a safe private place. How could you let this happen?"

I wrap my arms around her, stopping her rant and wearing a hole in the floor. "Mom, Mom… Listen. I wasn't caught, ok? It turns out it was a certain someone we've been looking for a long time for…" I pause for dramatic effect. I love messing with her about something like this. I feel it makes it more interesting. She stands there, staring at me impatiently and waiting for me to continue. She crosses her arms and taps her foot. "Well… Stop with the dramatic stuff already. It's getting tiring. Just spit it out!"

"It was the old man who cursed me eighteen years ago with that quill! I followed him and found where he lives."

Her eyes widen and she covers her mouth as she gasps. "Are you sure he didn't spot you? I can only imagine what would happen if he saw you and followed you back here." She says this so quickly I almost don't get all of what she said. She walks to the window and looks past the curtain, scanning around for who may be out there.

"I'm sure, Mom. I watched him go through the doors and close them behind him. Besides, I was behind the big trees, out of sight. He would have to have x-ray vision in order to see me. I was looking around the castle he went into and realized I have seen it before. It was one of the castles on my list. It was the first one I was going to check."

She turns to me, furrowing her brow and crosses her arms. "You were 'going to check?'" she says using air quotes. "Um... I don't think so. You are not going anywhere near that man. There's no telling what else he would do to you. He may have had a reason for cursing you and is just waiting for you to show up so he can snatch you away."

I give her a hug. I know this has been tough for her not knowing what would happen to me, but I *need* to know if there's a way to reverse what's been done.

"I *have* to do this, Mom. I understand it's dangerous, but I can't keep going through this every evening without at least trying to reverse it. It's tiring and hurts every single time. I don't think I could stand this for the rest of my life. Besides, graduation is in about two days, and I *really* don't want to worry about changing into this thing that evening."

Mom has that look on her face that tells me she's going back and forth on what to do. I know she wants the best for me and for me to be safe, but she also knows there's nothing she can do to stop me when I have my mind set. I have shown her time and time again growing up, when I decide to do something, there is no stopping me from achieving it.

She takes a deep, staggering breath before speaking, "Well, I guess there's nothing I can say or do. You're an adult now and you'll do what you want. I just want you to be safe. Please keep that in mind. I don't know what I'd do if I lost you." Tears trickle down her cheeks and I pull her into a hug and sway back and forth, assuring her that everything will be okay.

I lay in bed, staring up at the ceiling. I need to figure out how I'm going to move forward. Should I just confront him face to face and ask him why he did this and get him to cure what he's done? What if Mom was right and he *does* know where and who I am?

I need to come up with a better plan

tomorrow. I only have a day and a half to

figure it out before graduation. That's not

much time, but it's all I have to work with. I

guess I'll have a lot of work to do tomorrow.

I stand and walk to my computer,

powering it on. I need to go ahead with some

plans tonight since I'm short on time. I guess

if I don't figure it out and get it fixed by

graduation just plan around that evening so

nothing happens. I don't need my friends

worrying about me, so it's best to plan that

evening with them as a backup plan.

I glance at the clock and it's

10:45pm., I think I have a plan to get everything taken care of. Since graduation starts at six and ends at eight, that gives me about thirty minutes to get home before I change. However, I can leave the graduation a little early so I can go celebrate with my friends. Their names, like mine, are in the H's, so once we're done, we can leave as early as we can and get our celebration started before, I have to get home. I call E and J and let them know about what I'm planning for next Saturday. They thought it was a great idea.

"Well, since you have to do something at 9:00pm, why don't we do something when you're done? I mean hell, it's not like you have a curfew or anything. Your mom is cool like that," Jake says. He *does* have a point. Usually, my ordeal is over by ten and everything is fine until the next one.

"That sounds good. How about we meet at my house around 10:15 and go from there?" We finished setting up the plans and I place my phone on the nightstand. I lay back down put my hands under my head and stared up at the ceiling.

It feels like a weight has been lifted. Now I can sleep and focus on where to go from here.

'Dragonism- A sickness that causes a person to shift into a dragon nightly for the rest of their lives.'

The alarm buzzes, making me fall out of bed.

Shit! I really need to change the volume

on this fucking thing.

Well, I'm up now. I may as well

get ready. I get my clothes, go to the

bathroom, and straighten up my hair. I glance at the mirror to make sure everything's in place, it is. *Good.*

I look at my schedule today and I may have just enough time after school to head to Searles Castle before my change.

Walking through the doors of the school, I am met by an aggressive pat on the shoulders, making me jump.

"This is it! The last day of this hell-hole…" I turn to see Eli standing there with a shit-eating grin on his face, looking at my balled-up fist in surprise.

"Dude don't sneak up on me like that. You scared the shit out of me." He's lucky I didn't punch him. He holds up his hands in surrender. "Sorry, I'm just pumped that today's the last and final day of school. No longer will we be confined to this prison. We're officially adults now and after tomorrow, we'll be unleashed into the world."

Well, he *does* have a point. I don't blame him one bit for being excited. I wish I could have half the excitement he does, but thanks to this stupid curse, I can't. All my thoughts

are on trying to be rid of it.

"I know, right? Finally." That's all I

can come up with. Eli's brows form a *v* as

he tilts his head. His arms crossed in front of

him. "Are you really, ok? I thought you'd be

more excited. We've been looking forward

to this for many years and now it's finally

come."

"I *am* excited. I just have other

things on my mind, and I guess the

excitement's not getting through." I laugh

and Eli joins me, still looking a bit

concerned.

"Well, let's just get through today then

67

later we can celebrate," he says holding up

his hand for a high five.

"Tomorrow will be better but yeah, let's

celebrate," I tell him. He shrugs his

shoulders, and we do our lame 'cool guy'

handshake. "Sure dude, tomorrow."

"Sure, sounds great," I reply. I guess

I'm going to have to figure out some way

to get to that castle

before it's too late.

In the last period, I sit here at my desk

and stare at the clock, counting down to the

last minute. The dismissal bell rings and I

jump from my seat, grabbing my bag and racing out the door, never to see this place again. "Good luck and I hope you enjoy…" The teacher starts talking but I don't hear anything after that, because I'm already gone. I can assume what she was saying. She just wants to tell us to enjoy ourselves out there in the 'real world' and give us a speech about safety and humility and blah blah blah. I've heard teachers preach about what it's like in the 'adult world,' and I already have plans, if I can get rid of this stupid curse.

I walk out into the hallway and the kids are cheering, glad that school has finally ended. Heading for the

door, Eli meets me and wraps his arm

over my shoulder.

"Finally, school's out forever!"

he cheers as we walk out. He lets go

of me and heads to his car, saluting me

before he turns and hops in, leaving

for wherever he's going. Now to head

to that castle.

It's getting dark. When I left the
house, it was about seven o'clock. That
gives me roughly two hours before my
change to find that man. I know it's going
to be risky; that's why I brought it back up:
my trusty bow and arrow, so I can shoot
from a distance. Well, that's if I see him
coming.

Glancing around, I don't see any movement.
That's good; maybe he's inside. Slowly I
make my way to the entrance. I know I
should find another way in, but I don't

71

have time to go around the entire castle looking for another way. I need that time to look for the old man, or at least any clues to fix what's been done to me. I get to the entrance and carefully check the door. Luckily, it's unlocked and doesn't seem to make a sound when opened.

The space is dark. I first enter into what I believe is an entry way, with doors leading to an amazing foyer. To my left is a fireplace with a floral design carved into the outer edge. On both sides of the fireplace are thick swirled columns. The design definitely looks to be ancient, like this castle is over one hundred years old. To the right is what appears to be some kind of parlor room with a baby grand piano. I peek my head in and see a shadow at the writing desk.

That must be him! Pulling my head back into the foyer, I lean against the wall. Looking at the ceiling, I take a deep breath, trying hard to steel myself to face him and make him reverse what he's done. I square my shoulders and turn to the entrance of the parlor.

"I need you to reverse what you've done to me," I demand as I face the old man.

He turns in shock and stands to face me. "How dare you enter my home, demanding me to do something for you! I don't even know who you are," he exclaims, crossing his arms over his chest. Then he takes a harder look, squinting his eyes and taking a step closer.

"Wait a minute, I *do* know you, don't I?" Suddenly his eyes open wide, and his mouth drops open. He covers his mouth as he steps back. "Oh my! You're that boy, Tallon Harcrose, aren't you." I squint my eyes at him and step closer.

"Yes, I am, and I see you remember me after all. You did something to me when I was a baby, and when I turned eighteen, I started transitioning into a dragon. It started when I was out celebrating my birthday with my friends. I want you to reverse what you did. I'm fixing to graduate, and I have a lot to look forward to. I don't need this. It hurts too much and it's exhausting." He backs up closer to his desk where his notebook is. I notice a quill sitting beside it. I only see it for a second. What happens next is like something out of one of those Merlin movies. In a span of a second, he takes the quill and disappears.

"What the…" I look all around, and he's gone.

He just vanishes right before my eyes.

How is that possible?

I look back at the desk and see that the notebook is still in place. After looking around, I grab it and sit at the desk. *Maybe there's something in here that'll help me figure out how to reverse this mess.*

I flip through and I'm shocked. The entries in this notebook date back to 1905. This book is in impeccable condition! The first entry just goes on about the castle and how everything is going. The castle had just been built and the owners were moving in. *Wow, so this is the journal of the original owner's wife of this castle! That's*

awesome. I knew this castle was old,

but seeing this proves it. Now I just

need to find where he wrote about me

and if there's anything that explains

what happened. I flip through the

notebook and stop suddenly when I see

something familiar. "How did he know my

mother's name?"

September 24, 1998,

It was a beautiful day for a stroll in the

park. Gina had her baby boy, and they

were enjoying the scenery. Little does she

know what was in store. For on his 18th

birthday, that baby boy will have a change

77

unlike any other. Tallon Harcrose will be the second in a century to turn into a DRAGON.

Long ago, Mrs. Searles lost her baby girl to Dragonism. When little Scarlet Searles turned eighteen, she found herself transforming into a dragon and had been cursed to change back until she found someone who would love her. How could someone love a dragon? No one would be brave enough to try even if she had let him. Maybe if she had another dragon to love her, they both could be released from Dragonism and live ever after the rest of their days.

78

So that's what he's up to. He wants to fix me up with some dragon girl so they can reverse what happened to her. But how is 'Dragonism' even a thing? I've never heard of it before. Of course, I also thought dragons were fictional too, so there goes that.

Well, I know now why, and I guess how. But do I seriously need to find someone to love me in my dragon form in order to reverse this? That's easier said than done. Nowadays, if someone were to see me in my dragon

79

form, I would either be sent away to be

experimented on or locked away for

fear of danger. Just as I think that's the

end, I flip to the last page…

"IN CASE THE QUILL GETS LOST,

USE THIS MAP AND DRAGON

PENDANT TO SCRIBE FOR IT. THE

PENDANT WILL LEAD THE WAY."

A folded map along with what looks

like a necklace with a little dragon charm

on it appears. I put down the notebook and

unfolded the map. It appears to be a map of

the earth.

Eeerrrkk. I hear a door squeak open. I

quickly refold the map and shove it and the

pendant into my pocket. I shut the

notebook and sneak into a dark corner of

the room by the door. If whoever is nearby

enters the room, I'll be able to slip out

really quickly. Footsteps echo behind me

and disappear down the hall. I poke my

head out into the foyer and look. No one is

around. Glancing towards the door, I make

my way out as quietly as I can.

Chapter Six

Luckily, I made it out and went back to the cave just in time. I look at my watch and it's five minutes till nine. I get to the back of the cave and start preparing for the transition. I take my clothes off and settle in for a long agonizing evening.

When I get home the next morning, I start getting to work setting up the map. I need to find out where that old man and quill are. Where could they have gone?

I grab the necklace and hold it above the map. *Please let this work. Please let this work.* This better not be some kind of trick to throw me off. Otherwise, why would he just leave that book behind? Could it be a way to lead me away from him?

Suddenly the dragon pendant starts to glow purple and circle around a city. It lands with a thud, like a magnet when it finds metal. Looking closer at the map, a

83

flood of emotions floods my system.

Manchester, New Hampshire. That's not too far from here. Somehow, it's familiar. I don't know what it is about this place, but it brings emotions out that I didn't know I had.

"Okay, now all I need to do is make the trip." Folding the map, I place it and the pendant in my go- bag. I've already started packing for whatever trip comes up after high school, so I won't be dragging too much with the packing.

The door opens and Mom pops her head in. "Hey sweet boy. How's it going?" She looks a bit apprehensive. I wave her in. "Come look at this." I pull the map and pendant out. "I found these in that castle, and it shows me where the quill and stuff are."

Her eyes widen and eyebrows crease. "I know this is a stupid question as you are right here in front of me, but are you okay? Did you find that man?" She bombards me with questions, but I don't blame her. I'd probably be the same way if I was in her shoes. "Yes, he was there. I confronted him and all he did was just disappear. He *did* recognize me, but then he just vanished." I tell her about the journal and what was written in it; how I may not be the only one afflicted with this curse. "He wants to pair me up with Scarlet Searles," I explain. "She's the daughter of Edward Searles, the original owner of that castle. Apparently, she was cursed by that quill almost a hundred years ago, and the only way to reverse it is for her to find a male dragon to mate with. Then they will be free." She's rendered speechless. Her mouth opens and closes but nothing comes out.

I place my arm around her shoulder for comfort. "I know, Mom. I know. Apparently, the way to find that quill is with this map and pendant. He didn't go far. He's in Manchester."

Her eyes widen and she covers her

mouth. "Please don't tell me you're going to do what I think you're going to do." Her voice strains with every word. I put her head in my hands. "I must. I can't live like this for the rest of my life. I need to find that quill and figure out how to reverse this. There *has* to be a way." I try my best to settle her nerves, but nothing I do or say seems to help. Eventually she relents and although I know she really doesn't want me to go, I feel I have to, and she knows it.

Graduation day finally arrived and went off without a hitch. We threw our caps in the air and cheered to another chapter finally coming to an end. We did as planned and got out of there with plenty of time to spare for fun before the dreaded time of the night.

When our celebrating is over, we say our goodbyes and part ways. I tell the guys I plan on doing some traveling of my own. They are thrilled. I guess in their way, they've been worried about me since my birthday and seemed to be relieved to know I won't be staying home and wasting my new freedom. Little do they know the plans I have aren't going to be as fun as they thought. I'm all packed and ready to go. I looked it up, and there's a really nice apartment in that area within my price range.

All that's left to do is to find a job.

"Please call me when you get there. Don't forget you have your savings…" Mom's voice is wary as she smooths her hands down my arms.

"Don't worry, Mom," I interrupt, placing my hands on her shoulders. "I'll be fine. I'll call and I will be smart about it. You taught me well; I know what to do." Tears stream down her face and she wraps me in a warm hug. She kisses me goodbye on the cheek and with that, I'm off to Manchester.

I walk into the apartment building. It's decent and pre-furnished, which is wonderful. A grey sofa and loveseat face the wall of windows. I look to my left and there's a kitchen big enough to fit a family of ten. Chrome and black appliances seem to be the theme. I shut the door behind me and make my way around, finding a master bedroom with an ensuite bathroom.

I place my bags next to the dresser and walk to the living room. Standing at the wall of windows overlooking the city of Manchester, I contemplate what to do next. "Where are you?" I mumble to myself. I know he's here somewhere. It's too bad the pendant doesn't pinpoint the exact location; it just tells the city or town. I *am* grateful for the approximate location, but it would be nice to find out where exactly he is.

I get my phone out and call Mom. "Hey Mom, I made it," I say as soon as she answers. She lets out a breath that I hadn't realized she was holding. I guess Mom worries more than I thought.

"That's great to hear. So, tell me, how it is so far? How was the trip?" She shoots question after question. I fill her in on the trip and end the call, telling her I will talk to her later.

I place the pendant around my neck

and head out the door. He *must* be here somewhere.

Well, I've been in this town for nearly three years and nothing! Not a damn thing has made this stupid fucking pendant glow, move, or do a damn thing. The only upside to being here is the fact that I was able to start my own marketing business. Manchester, New Hampshire is definitely the place to be to begin a marketing career.

As I walk down the street, a gorgeous

woman catches my eye. 'Diamond Dave's' flashes bright above the door at the restaurant she is walking towards. I check my watch and realize it's lunchtime, so I walk towards the restaurant. Not long after I enter, the pendant starts to glow. I pull it out of my shirt, taking a closer look.

Suddenly, someone crashes into me. "Oh, my goodness. I'm so sorry," a feminine voice exclaims. Looking up, I realize the gorgeous woman from the street is standing before me, looking embarrassed. God help me, she looks so hot all flustered.

I pull out my phone, hoping to lighten the mood, "Don't worry, I wasn't paying attention, are you okay? These things can be dangerous," I ask, holding up my phone. She looks me up and down, making me feel stupid. Maybe it was a poor joke. "Sorry, that wasn't as funny as it was in my head." I put the phone back in my pocket. "No! It *was* funny, I'm so sorry I've been a bit distracted today." Her cheeks flush a sexy pink. I just hope she doesn't have a boyfriend.

"I hope I'm not being too forward, but you can make it up to me by going out on a date with me Friday at seven." I take a card out of my pocket and give it to her, bringing out the charm to entice her to accept.

"Here's my number. Give me a call if you want." I head for the door, hopeful about Friday.

Walking down the road, a thought crosses my mind. *What if seven is too late?* Shit! I need to figure out how to cover for the fact that I am cursed from her. There's no telling how she'd react or how it would turn out.

Walking back into my apartment, I sit on the couch facing the wall of windows. I lean my head back and stare at the ceiling. "I got it! I'll just set an alarm for eight thirty. Now I just need to know whether she's interested in me or not. Given the way she

95

was blushing today, I feel like I may have a shot."

I walk to the window. I need to decide where to go tonight when I shift. All I see are city buildings all around. I look at my watch; I still have a few hours before my shift. That'll give me enough time to find a place.

As I walk around the town of Manchester, I look and find a trail at the edge of what looks to be woods.
There has to be a cave or something there. I start for the wooded area. I walk through soft grass up to my knees. Looking up, the darkening sky peaks between the trees. That

96

girl I met at the restaurant today crosses my mind. *She looked so familiar. Where have I seen her before?* I walk a little bit further into the woods and to my right is what looks to be a hole inside of a mountain. *A cave?* Walking closer, I look around. *Yeah, it definitely looks like a cave.* I walk further in, and it is so spacious.

A lot bigger than the cave back home. The ceiling looks to be about fifteen to twenty feet at least, big enough for me to shift and have plenty of room to move. Feeling confident in the space for the evening, I head back.

Later, after a long and tiring night of wandering around in the cave, I'm finally on my way home. As I reach the door, my phone rings. I answer it immediately, hoping it was her. "Hey, so you decided to take me up on my offer?" I ask, praying that I'm right.

"How did you know it was me? I didn't even say anything yet," she replies, and I thank all things holy that it was who I was hoping for. She sounds a little creeped out. I guess I need to put her out of her misery before she thinks I am crazy.

"Okay, I didn't actually know. I was just hoping it was you. If it wasn't, I would've worked something

out." I can't help but laugh at the situation.

"Anyway…" she says, breaking the not

so uncomfortable silence. "I would love to

go out with you Friday." I smile. "Glad to

hear it. I'll pick you up at seven." Silence

follows. She starts breathing a little heavier.

"Sounds good. I can't wait! So… what are

you wearing?" She slurs. *Is she drunk?* I

can't help but laugh. I hope she has someone

sober with her or something. "Why do you

want to know what I'm wearing? Are you

okay?" I hear the sexiest sound come from

the other end. She starts giggling. "I…I'm

soorrryy. I'm fffine. I have some…one to

gggive…me a ride home. I'll see you Fridddday" She struggles to get the words out, slurring as she speaks. Perhaps I should go make sure she's really okay.

I do a little research on the way out and the only bar around is a place called Dolly's. I arrive just in time to see her being helped into a car by a woman. *Well, that makes me feel a little better. You should follow her…* A voice in my head says. What the hell?? *Where did you come from?* I ask the voice in my head. *I'm the dragon part of you. Adilyne is* The One. *She will help you to come to terms with who you are. I have been apart from you all these years. I am only able to*

speak now due to Adilyne Grace showing up
again in your/our life. I shake my head, not
ready for all of this insane shit right now.
Adilyne's ride pulls out and I follow after her. I
need to be sure she arrives home safely.

Once we get to what I assume is her
apartment, I sit and watch as she stumbles
out of the car. I want so badly to run to her
and help, but the driver runs to her aid and
helps her to the door, and with a few more
stumbles, she makes her way inside her
house.

I sit here for a minute; I feel an odd
sensation come over me. Something about

101

this woman seems so familiar. Have we met before?

We have *met her before,* my dragon says, *when you were a child. I wasn't in existence yet, but I retain your memories. Obviously, my recollection is a shit ton better than yours.* I roll my eyes. This is going to get annoying really quick. I headed home after seeing the lights go out in her apartment. It brings my mind at ease knowing she is safe.

Chapter Seven

I sit next to the window, coffee in hand, staring out over the city. It really is nice up here. *Ah!* I grab my chest, feeling pain shoot out. I rub and feel scales. *What in the actual fuck is happening to me? We are becoming one,* he hisses. *Pretty soon, we will share the same body, unless you find a way to reverse*

103

what has happened. What do you mean we will become one? Aren't we one in the same already? Now this is really confusing me. Does that mean I will cease to exist? My dragon sighs in annoyance. *We simply coexist at the moment. When we become one, you will be able to bring me to the surface anytime. You won't be forced to bring me to the surface at a certain time of day. However, if you reverse what has been done, I will leave, and you will be free of me. The choice is ultimately up to you. I have no say in the matter.*

That gives me a lot to think about. Do I want to be stuck with this dragon for the rest of my life? I'm not sure. I need time to think. *How much time do we have?* I sense him mulling it over. *Roughly two months' time. You need to make the decision pretty quick, or it will be made for you.*

I walk back to the kitchen and put my now empty cup in the sink. All this is too much, too fast. Two months? That's not much time at all. I grabbed my joggers and a T-shirt. I need to run it out, to get fresh air.

I run for God only knows how far. The cool morning breeze feels great on my face. This is just what I needed. I look around and recognize the area. Adilyne lives on this block. I jog further down and look up at her building, just in time to see her in what looks like her bathroom, splashing water on her face. Holy fuck, she is so beautiful.

Looking at my watch, I grin when I see it's Friday. My heart beats faster in my chest, knowing in just about twelve hours, I will be sweeping her off her feet.

Get your head out of your ass. There's no time to gawk. You have a lot to do before tonight, my dragon side reminds me. *Okay, chill. I have an idea of where we're going this evening. It'll all be ready by the time I pick her up.* Turning around, I jog back towards

106

my house. Stopping mid jog, a thought crosses my mind. I don't officially know where she lives. I pull out my phone and shoot her a quick text. *What's your address?* A bubble with dots appear, telling me she is typing. *That's right, you might want to know where I live. 114 Maple Way, Manchester, NH. I can't wait.* She responds with a heart emoji. I text my response, then throw my phone back in my pocket. There's a lot to do to prepare for tonight.

The restaurant has been booked, and the suit has been chosen. *See, it didn't*

take too long to get stuff ready for tonight. I feel as if the dragon inside me rolls his eyes.

You still needed time to get those done. Without time, you would not have accomplished so much. It's my turn to roll my eyes. He's already starting to get on my nerves.

I glance at my watch. It's getting closer to the time I'm meant to pick up Adilyne. Pulling out my phone, I set an alarm. I need to be sure I make it out of there with plenty enough time to get to the cave to turn.

After checking to make sure I have
108

everything, I make my way out the door. *I should grab some flowers on my way. I need to make a good first impression, I don't want to screw it up.* I haven't been on many dates on account of my current situation. *Sounds good to me. Don't fuck it up. This may be the only chance you have, my dragon sneers.* I feel like he's mocking me now.

Getting in my souped-up Chevy Camero SS with a 6.2-liter engine, I grin as I buckle up. I've always wanted something with a lot of power and when I could afford it, I went for it. I put it into drive and headed to Adilyne's.

Arriving at her door, flowers in hand, I pull my hand through my hair and smooth out any strands that may have strayed. I knock on the door, nerves shooting through me. The door opens and the most stunning woman I have ever laid my eyes on stands on the other side, her shimmering light grey eyes looking me up and down. I handed the flowers to her. "These are for you," I stammer. "You look stunning."

Her cheeks flush the same color as the roses as I kiss her soft cheek. "Thank you. These are lovely flowers. Please come in while I find a vase for them," she offers as I step into her apartment, shutting the door behind me. I turn, watching as she walks to

her kitchen. The way she moves so

confidently around brings something out in

me. I almost don't want her to turn around

too quickly, I'm enjoying the view.

She reaches up and pulls a vase out

of the cabinet. I can't take my eyes off her.

Every move she makes calls to me; all I want

to do is sweep her in my arms and have my

way with her. She walks towards me, a shy

smile pulling at her kissable lips. "Are you

ready?" she asks, and I nod. I know I am.

I'm ready to show her a good time. She

grabs my waiting hand. I gently rub the back

of her hand as we walk towards my car. I

can't believe how lucky I am.

We walked to the passenger side, and I open the door for her. My mom always taught me to be courteous and gentlemanly to ladies; they will respect you for it. I've always opened doors for her and now is not any different. "M'lady," I say as I wave her into the car.

As soon as she's settled, I hop in and start for Ristorante Massimo. It's one of the most romantic places I've seen in my research of restaurants within a hundred-mile radius.

Suddenly, it hits me as I stare at the road ahead. What if I can't fix what has been done? What happens if I run out of time and I'm permanently a shifter? I

don't know how I'm going to live like that.

We will figure it out, my dragon

chimes in. *Whatever comes, we will deal with it. If you were to choose to keep me around, which is what I hope you choose, you will have the choice when to let me roam. You will also be with me when I fly. Essentially, you will be free. I still don't know what I want to choose. That* does sound appealing but what if I get found out? What about the dragon that I'm supposedly 'meant' for?

"Penny for your thoughts?" Adilyne

113

quips, breaking me from my reverie. I smile at her. "I'm just thinking about how beautiful you look this evening." She flushes crimson, giving me the sexiest smile, before looking out the window.

Tonight, you don't need to worry yourself about what is to become. Enjoy yourself and the beauty beside us. I guess he's right. I just need to enjoy the moment before it's over.

Once at the restaurant, I quickly hop out and go for Adilyne's door. Opening it, I reach my hand to her for support, which she accepts. "Thank you," she says. I bow in jest. "No problem. It's my pleasure."

The valet walks up and I hand him the keys. We make our way in the impressive brick building, and we are led to our table.

A cheerful brunette approaches the table. "Good evening, my name is Jenelle, and I will be your server this evening. Can I get you started with a drink?" We ordered our drinks and I stare at Adilyne. I cannot believe how beautiful she is. I just hope I don't fuck it up. I've had small relationships before. But of course, I was in high school, and they really didn't mean much. I feel such a pull towards Adilyne. I feel like I know her from somewhere. I need to find out more about who she is, maybe then I will get to the bottom of it. She looks at me, her expression like an adorable lost puppy. "So, I guess I'll start some sort of conversation," I tease. She answers with a flush of her cheeks and a soft smile. "Tell me about yourself, what do you do for a living?"

A smile grows and she perks up. She tells me all about how she first moved here from Windham, which is where I moved from. I'm intrigued. I need to know more. She goes on to tell me how she has moved up in her career and now she's on her way to becoming an editor at a big publishing company. "That's great!" I exclaim. "I'm so happy for you. It's always good when you get closer to living your

dream. It took me a few years, but I'm

finally there."

She tells me more about her childhood and

where she came from. I just cannot believe

that we lived in the same area and we're just

meeting now. When she talks, it's hard to

focus on the words. All I can do is to watch

her beautiful full lips as she talks about her

passions.

BING BING BING, my alarm sounds

scaring the bejesus out of the both of us. I

dig my phone out of my pocket and hit the

stop alarm button. "Wow, it's already eight

thirty? Time flies when you're having fun."

I quip with a smile. Standing, I extend my hand to her.

Adilyne smiles and takes it, scooting out of the seat. I take some cash out of my wallet and set it on the table. "That should take care of the bill and tip. Are you ready?" She nods. Still holding her hand, we walked out.

The ride to her house is quiet. I glance over at her, and it seems as though she's about to cry. What's going on in her mind? Did she not have a good time? It sure seemed like it was going so well.

When we finally get back to her apartment, I walk her to the door. Her head

118

stays down the entire time. I need to make this up to her. I need to show her I *can* be a fun date. "I had fun. I hope to see you again." I really do. I'd hate for it all to end here.

She forces a smile. "I had a good time too." I can tell she meant it. But if she had such a good time, then why does she look so distraught?

Chapter Eight

I lean on the door after she is safely inside and lay my head back against it. *What went wrong? She said she had a good time, but I could tell something was off.*

I feel my dragon surge inside. *It didn't help that you set your alarm, you jack wad.*

120

There were other options. She most likely thought you were not interested in her enough and maybe you just wanted a way out.

I take a deep breath, push myself off the door and headed towards my car. *Perhaps you're right. I need to make it up to her somehow.* I glance at the time. Shit! I only have ten minutes to get to the cave before I turn.

After getting to the cave, I start preparing for the evening. My dragon growls, *I need to*

121

spread my winds some. Night after night, we

are couped up in this god forsaken cave.

That doesn't sound too bad, although I'm

not sure if it's a great idea. *What if we're*

seen? There could be some concerns... You

always worry about nothing. What are they

going to do if they do *see us, fly over, and*

capture us? he snickers. *Actually, yes, they*

could if they had time. They could just get a

helicopter or something. I feel him roll his

eyes. *Fine, just for tonight, we can see how*

it goes. But if things go south... ... Yeah,

yeah, yeah, he answers, interrupting me. I

shift, then off we fly out of the cave.

I see through my dragon's eyes. The

sight is so magnificent. We soar above the trees,

122

and I see colors of gold, green and red. You can tell fall is in the air. *This is what I'm talking about. You see how free and serene it feels? It's in a dragon's nature to be out in the wild, to feel the wind in their scales.* I have to admit that he's right. From the research I've done and from what I can tell, dragons have always been skyward unless they are sleeping, eating, or resting. From my experience this evening, I can see why. It feels amazing to be up here away from everything, flying above and between the mountains. Someone would have to have amazing sight to be able to see us up here.

Roughly an hour later we come in for a landing inside the cave, just in time for the shift back into my human form. *Okay, you have a point. I think it would be better to fly at night. It's freeing and makes the time go by so much faster.*

After arriving home, I run through what might be needed to be the best date to win Adilyne back.

"Okay," I say aloud to myself. "When we were getting to know each other, she told me how much she loves historical sights."

I sit up from my position on the couch. "That's it! She has dreams of becoming an

124

editor one day, which could mean that she loves to read. It only makes sense to take her to one of the places I know that has a pretty great library in it." I've visited the castle from time to time, trying and failing to find the quill and ended up finding a library in one of the towers.

My dragon huffs. *First, you have to convince her to go on another date with you, then yeah go for it.* I roll my eyes. Sometimes he can be a big pain in the ass.

In my opinion, hiking gives almost

125

the same kind of feeling as flying. The cool air around you along with the smell of fall hitting the senses. I take a break next to the creek, taking in the beauty that surrounds me. It really is serene up here. No one to bother you, no city noise, all worries subsiding when you're surrounded by all of this.

I kneel at the water and reach down, feeling the coolness flow through my fingers. I feel something tickle my chest, and suddenly a shimmer nearly blinds me in the water. Rubbing my chest, a scar has taken the place of what used to be a scale. *What is going on? Am I shedding or something?* I ask the only one that would know. *It has begun. You are starting to shed off the scales as we become one. Once you lose all of them, it's only a matter of time before we are united. I still need to find that quill. It's dangerous out there, especially in the hands of that man. No matter what I choose, it needs to be found.*

I skim the water, needing to find that scale. The last thing I need is someone to find it, do some sort of DNA check, and find out my secret.

"What do you think you're doing? Why are you following me?" I turn to see Adilyne marching up to me. My eyebrows shoot straight up. I quickly readjust my shirt, not wanting the scar left from the scale out for show. "Uh... Hey, Adilyne. I didn't know you were even here," I stammer in surprise. "I swear, I'm not following you. I come up here most weekends when I get a chance. It's so serene here, it gives me the time to clear my head and get away from it all."

Her face drops and her cheeks turn red. She shakes her shoulders, seeming to shake off the embarrassment. "I am so sorry, I just dug myself a hole, I'm going to go dig myself out now," Adilyne murmurs, turning to leave. I can't help but laugh. That's quite an interesting way of making light of a situation. It makes me adore her even more.

I reach out and grabbed her shoulder. I can't

let her leave. "Wait, don't go," I plead, and

she stops "I need to apologize for the other

night. I feel as though I did something to

upset you. How can I make it up to you?"

Adilyne's eyes reflect her hurt. "Well,

first of all, you can tell me why you had to

set an alarm on your phone knowing you had

a date. I thought it was going well, then the

alarm went off and suddenly we had to go."

Shit, I knew it! I should've known that

was going to come back and bite me in the

ass. I need to come up with something. I

can't very well tell her the truth. No one

needs to know that.

Just tell her it was a family emergency. There's no explanation necessary, people are generally gullible like that, the dragon chimes in.

"There was a family emergency I had to deal with, so I set the alarm so I could have time to spend time with you before tending to family matters. I should've gone about it differently, though. I'm truly sorry," I insist. "I would love to make it up to you." She seems to thaw a little and then a smile lights up her face. "I would love that," she replies, and then we set up a date for the Friday after next. I'm not exactly ready to show her the castle yet. I need to save that for after I really make it up to her. I would hate to show her that place only for her to dump me for someone better.As she walks away, I stare at her retreating figure. She's so damn beautiful. I can't believe she gave me another chance after what happened. I watch as her ass moves side to side in those tight shorts. It's like she knows I'm watching her. She moves with such purpose. I bite my lip, biting back the urge to take her somewhere and do things that could rock her world.

When she disappears out of sight, I give up on trying to look for that fucking scale. It's long gone by now. I just hope it doesn't come back to bite me in the ass later.

Chapter Nine

The time has come. My second shot at impressing Adilyne. As I reach her door, the necklace with the pendant starts to shimmer in my jacket pocket. *What the hell? That's only supposed to happen...*

My eyes shot up towards the door. "No,

that cannot be." It's not possible. How?

Words fail me. Confusion floods my system.

How can the quill be here?! Why would

Adilyne have it? The shimmer subsides as

she opens the door. All thoughts fail as I lay

eyes on her. The way the dress on her hugs

all her curves in all the right places is

esmerizing. I cleared my throat and handed

her the white and red roses. "You look

stunning." That seems to be the only thing

my dumbass can manage. Her cheeks flush

crimson as she takes the flowers.

After putting them up, we headed out to

Firefly. From what I've seen, it's another

133

romantic restaurant around here. The other one looked to be Italian inspired, this one appeared to be more Tuscan-inspired.

"I'm glad you decided to give me another chance. I promise not to screw it up this time," I joke. Adilyne reaches across and takes hold of my hand, resting on the gear shift. "Me. Too. Next time something happens, don't be afraid to tell me. I'll understand." She smiles, then turns her head to look out the window. As we walk through the glass doors, we are greeted and brought to our seats. We order our drinks; I cannot keep my eyes off Adilyne as she looks at the menu. Her chestnut brown hair, long and beautiful, is pulled up in a half updo, two strands curled down framing her face. She went subtle with her makeup, the color of her grey eyes popping against the light blue of her eyelids. The more I stare, the more familiar she seems. Where do I know her from?

Suddenly it hits me. Throughout middle school, I had a best friend, a girl who I thought I loved. I was heartbroken when she told me her family was moving, that she had to leave. That girl was Adilyne! My heart picks up a beat.

That's why I'm so drawn to her! She's the one that got away. I feel the need to scream

135

for joy, but I settle on internalizing it with my Dragon. *I knew you would figure it out, eventually.* Seriously? He really gets on my nerves. I roll my eyes.

Just then, Adilyne looked up at me. "So, did everything turn out okay? You said you had to deal with stuff after our date, I hope it went well," she asks, her arms resting on the table. I give her enough information to satisfy her. I blow out a breath once the waitress comes and takes our order.

We sit there for the remainder of the evening catching up on different things. She

136

still doesn't seem to know about when we were younger, and I don't tell her. I need her to figure it out herself.

Standing at her front door, I step closer to her.

She smells so enticing. I wrap my arms around her,pulling her close. She welcomes my touch by wrapping her arms around my neck. Taking this as a sign, I kiss her, moving a hand to her cheek and deepening the kiss. She returns it with fervor, tasting like heaven and wine.

When we finally come up for air, I rest

my forehead against hers. Adilyne smiles as she offers, "I really had a great time tonight. Thank you so much for a fantastic evening."

I wrap my arms around her, never wanting to let go. "It's my pleasure." I smile and kiss her once more before we say our goodbyes.

I make sure Adilyne makes it inside safely, then I return to my car. Glancing at my watch, I realize I only have twenty minutes to get to the cave, or at least somewhere isolated for my shift. Hopping in the car, I speed off to a secluded location.

I start thinking about the dilemma I'm faced with; the dreaded decision on whether to find the quill and end this nightmare once and for all, or let the time run out, which will cause my dragon and I to become one in the same. I know this option will end with me being able to shift any time I choose. As time goes on, it's getting easier to choose. The more time I spend with him, the harder it seems it will be to get rid of him. I feel like he's already becoming a part of me. *The process has started, so you might want to choose now.*

I nod, knowing full well it does no good. *You're right. I do need to choose. But another dilemma popped up. Adilyne. Let's say I choose to remain with you, how will she feel about dating a dragon? Will she freak out? Will she turn me in to be experimented on?*

Listen, ... he starts. Oh great, a speech is coming. I roll my eyes. *Will you listen, you intolerant jackass? Alright, we know the quill is out there. We still have to get it, no matter what you decide. Second, and most importantly, she is not the kind of person to watch as people take you away. We both*

140

saw the look in her eyes as you were saying goodnight. She is falling for you; she just doesn't know it yet.

We fly for another thirty minutes then return to the cave. Perhaps it wouldn't be so bad if I fully became a dragon shifter. It's so freeing when we're
flying and I wouldn't mind at all doing that every night, or at least every so often when I choose. I just hope Adilyne will be okay with it.

I arrive home and sit on the couch facing the window. I need to figure out how I'm going to find that damned quill before anyone else suffers at the hands of it.

Staring in the distance of the

darkened sky, a thought pops into my head.

What if I go back to the castle and look once

more? I'm bound to find something I missed.

On the other hand, the pendant glowed when

I was at Adilyne's house. Is there any

chance the quill is there? No, it can't be.

How can she have it?

I throw my head back and stare at the

ceiling. I need to figure this out fast.

Standing at the castle doorway, I

take a deep breath and push the doors open.

Quiet is the only thing that greets me inside.

It doesn't seem like anyone is here. That's a

142

good sign. I start looking; maybe I'll find

some sort of clue as to where it could be.

I turn the corner down the hall, and I

notice steps. I follow them. When I get to

the top, I'm met by a door with a Fleur-De-

Lis symbol on it. The symbol is black with

gold glitter in it. It's enticing. I grab the

knob, which is also as impressive as the

symbol. It's a crystal looking knob with gold

flaking around the base.

I push open the door to find a library

filled with books that seem to be over a

hundred years old.

Adilyne would love this room. It's definitely

the right choice to take her here. She's been

143

telling me how much she loves books and editing. I should bring her here and show her this library.

A writing desk sits under one of the windows facing a garden. I look out the window and notice it appears to be a rose garden that seems like it's been tended to recently. Has that man been back? That must mean he's still around. That gives me some hope at least. I'll still be able to get to him and get that quill.

I look at the desk and see the notebook I've become all too familiar with, the one he used to write

the stories in with the quill. I need to see if

he's caused any more harm to anyone.

I flip through it. Nothing. Well, that's a good sign. He hasn't wreaked any havoc on anyone else. I put it back and turned towards the door. *There's nothing here. At least I know that he's still coming here, which means he's close.* I just need to figure out where the hell he is.

We will fly tonight and see if we find him or something that will lead us to him. He's bound to show up, my dragon replies as we start down the road.

Chapter Ten

We have been flying for almost an hour and nothing. Where the fuck is he? We've been flying in and

around the city, thank fuck everyone seems to be asleep. Otherwise, they'd see us, and a shit ton of trouble would follow. *I believe I may have spotted him,* my dragon states as we start for the edge of the wood. We fly closer, staying far enough away so as to not be spotted. As we get closer, I realize it's not him. *No, it's not him, go back to the cave before he sees us!*

That was too close for comfort. *Next time, try and be more careful. If he would've looked up, we*

would've been seen, and God only knows what

would've happened, I growl as I shift back and take control.

My dragon rolls his eyes. *Take a chill pill. That was far from happening. I know what I'm doing. If you want to find him,*

147

you'll have to have more trust in me.

I take a deep breath and head back to my car. This is getting fucking ridiculous. I'm running out of time. The longer he's out there with that damned thing, the higher the chances someone else could get hurt. I need to find it now.

It's been about three weeks and I have come close too many times to count. I've gone back to the castle and almost caught him. If I'd gone there a little earlier, I would've caught the bastard. He seems to

148

slip away too soon. It seems like he goes there at a certain time each day but just when I think he will be there, he changes it up. It's like he knows I'm trying to get to him.

I just need a break from all this bullshit and plan something out for Adilyne. It's been too long since we last went out and I need to feel her next to me. An idea pops in my head. *I'll take her on a picnic, then to the castle. She'll love the library. It'll be right down her alley.* I feel his agreement.

After picking the best spot to have the picnic, I dial Adilyne's number. "Hello?" she answers, seeming a bit shaken, like she

149

got the shit scared out of her.

"Hey Adilyne, it's Tallon. Do you have any

plans for Saturday?" There's no reason to beat around the bush. May as well get it out now.

"Oh, hey Tallon!" She perks up when she realizes it's me. Dear God, I love hearing my name on her lips. "Not that I'm aware of. Why?" "I have a surprise for you, and I'd love to take you out. Just wear something pretty and comfortable and I'll pick you up at eleven thirty." I hear her breath on the other end. The need for her to be with me gets stronger each moment I'm not with her.

"That sounds great. So, what's the surprise?" She tries to get the details, but my lips are zipped shut. There's no way I'm going to tell. "You'll just have to see Saturday," I tease. I smile, knowing the not knowing is driving her crazy.

She relents, "Fine, don't tell me." I sense her smile on the other end, and it makes me smile in return. "See you then." I throw my phone beside me on the couch and sit back my head resting on the back. *Don't take too long of a break, Tallon. Remember, the longer he is out there, the higher the*

151

probability of more trouble. I roll my eyes as I hop off the couch. *I know, there's no need to remind me. I know what's at stake.* He doesn't have to nag my ass off like a fucking mother. I swear he worries more than my own mother. I'll go by the castle one last time, and maybe this time I'll get lucky.

I take a deep breath, steeling myself for the disappointment of the stranger not being here yet again and continuing this never-ending cycle of the ridiculous game of hide and seek.

Walking through the doors,

something changes in the air. Movement

captures my attention down the hall, and I

hurry in that direction. I turn the corner to

find someone's cloak trailing behind as they

go in one of the rooms. I follow; that's got

to be him. I've never seen anyone else step

foot here in all the years I've been coming.

I enter the room and find the old man

standing there, his hands tucked into the

sleeves of his cloak.

"Finally, you came," he says as I walk

closer. It's like he was expecting me.

"Are you serious? Finally?" I shout.

"I've been looking for you for years, ever

153

since you disappeared." I pull out the pendant and hold it up. "I used this to track you back to Manchester and yet, you seriously think I 'finally came?'" I can't believe the pair on this ass.

He smiles, a sickly yellow smile. Then he starts laughing. "You see, Tallon, you try far too hard." He takes his hands out of the sleeves and opens his arms wide. "I have been here the entire time. That pendant you've grown so fond of is just to track the quill. The magic in both the quill and the pendant are linked. One does not exist without the other."

He puts his hands back in the

154

sleeves. Is he some kind of rejected monk or something? I've only seen monks standing like that.

"Then why isn't the pendant active now? If, as you said, 'one doesn't exist...' then why is it not glowing or anything?" Then the image of the pendant glowing in front of Adilyne's door pops into my head. My eyes widen as I look at his growing smile.

"Oh, now he's getting it! The quill no longer remains in my possession. It has been passed down to someone else who has the gift to wield it. My time is almost up, and the story must go on..." His words fade

155

as he starts to disappear again.

I run towards him. "No! I'm not done with you yet." But I'm too late. He's gone. What the fuck am I going to do now?

Chapter Eleven

What the hell am I going to do? The old man is gone and not only that, supposedly the woman I've been dating is the one who is destined for the magic of the quill.

My dragon rumbles. *There's only one*

thing to do. You need to get that quill from

Adilyne. With magic like that, she could

subconsciously hurt others or worse, hurt

herself. I take a deep breath and rest my head

against the headrest in my car. *I know. I just*

don't want to hurt her by doing it. I can't

just ask for it without telling her why. I need

to find a way to get it from her without her

even knowing.

Friday comes and goes without a hitch. We

fly through the air; the cool breeze melting away

some of the anxiety from before. With the dark

sky above and the trees below, I feel a sense of

peace before the inevitable storm. I know it's

going to be hard and excruciating, but I need to

get that quill away from Adilyne somehow,

before something happens to her. I just found her

again, I'm not going to lose her to the thing that

made my life hell.

We land and I turn. I need to prepare for

tomorrow. I need to show her how I feel and

prove that what I'm about to do is for her.

Saturday finally arrives and my nerves

get the better of me. Grabbing the basket, I

place it in the back seat then headed inside to

get Adilyne.

I grabbed the handkerchief out of my

pocket. I don't want her to see what I have

in store for her just yet. The pendant starts to

glow again, alerting me to the quill, which

159

must be in her apartment. I knock on the door.

Once she opens the door, she starts questioning me about the handkerchief in my hands. I just smile. "I told you I had a surprise for you. This..." I hold up the kerchief, "is because I don't want you to see until we get there." Her brow crinkles with apprehension.

"Don't worry, I won't put it on you until we get to the car. I'm not crazy," I laugh. There's no telling what's going on in her head.

When we get to my car; I have her turn around. I breathe in her scent, watermelon,

160

floral and Adilyne, such an intoxicating combination. I kiss her under her ear before putting the blindfold on. She takes a deep breath, leaning into me. I'd love to keep her against me like this, and if the time's right we might get back to it later, but right now, there's the surprise I have for her.

I look over to Adilyne. She's so damn gorgeous I have no idea why I ever let her go. Of course, we were so young; little did I know something would come of it. I study her features. Her brown hair pulled up in an adorable bun, the way her full lips pull to the side when she's nervous. I place my hand on her thigh, and she sets her hand on top of

161

mine, holding my hand in hers. "We're almost there," I reassure her. She smiles and rests her head against the headrest. I scan the road, seeing the entrance of the park we grew up in coming into view.

I park next to the curb. Shit, I forgot about the steps leading up to the gazebo. I hurry out of the car and get to her side. Opening the door, I reach for her hand. "Careful, there's a curb right here, you'll have to step up." She bites her lip as she steps up on the curb. I guide her to the gazebo one step at a time.

"How long are you going to keep me in suspense? I don't know how much longer I

162

can take being in the dark," she explains.

"Don't worry we're almost there." I reassure

her. One more step.

Once we enter the gazebo, I face her

towards the picnic area I prepared. "Are you

ready?" I ask, nerves setting in. I hope she

likes it.

"I've been ready from the get-go," she

answers, so I remove her blindfold. Her face

brightens and her cheeks flush as she places

her hands on her chest. "Wow, I can't

believe you did all of this!"

She wraps her arms around me, and I

pull her in close. She looks up at me, her

eyes watering. I lean in and kiss her. She

deepens the kiss quickly As I grab the back of her head, enjoying her full lips on mine. Before this goes any further, I pull away, reluctantly. "I wanted to do something different. Come have a seat." I take her hand in mine and lead her to the blanket.

Grabbing a bottle out of the basket, I pop the top of the wine and pour our glasses. "So, what's the occasion?" she questions. I can tell she's not used to being treated like this. Who are the assholes she's dated in the past? Has she never gotten spoiled the way she should? She's a gorgeous woman who deserves to be treated like a damn queen. I shrug nonchalantly. "No occasion. It's a beautiful day and I wanted to spend it with a beautiful woman." I take out the food I've prepared, and we spend the next hour eating and enjoying each other's company. I cannot wait to show her what else I have planned today. If she thinks this is good, she'll love the castle.

Adilyne looks around at the scenery. "So, what made you pick this place? It looks familiar." I smile. "This is where I grew up. It holds special memories for me, and I wanted to share it with you." Suddenly her eyes widen, and she smiles in return. "I think I remember this place. I used to live just down the road. I would walk this way almost

165

every day on my way to school." It surprises me that she hasn't seemed to put two and two together. Does she even remember me? It doesn't seem like it.

"I spent most of my weekends here. My mom and I used to have picnics here a lot," I tell her. We share memories of when we were young. It doesn't seem as though she really remembers me, so I just ignore it. There's no use trying to get someone to remember the past.

Once we finish, we head out. I don't tell her where we're going; it'll make it that much more surprising when she sees for herself.

We drive for a while before turning down Range Road. I glance at Adilyne. She looks confused as she asks, "Where are we going?"

Reaching over, I take her hand in mine. I can tell she's getting a bit nervous "The day's not over yet. I have one more surprise for you." My heart races as we get closer.

We turn down Searles Road, the stretch of road going to the castle. I look to the side of Adilyne and see her eyes widen. "Is that what I think it is?!" she gasps as she points to our destination. I grin as I reply, "If you're thinking *Castle* then you would be right. That's the surprise." We pull into the stone gateway, and I park. Rushing to her

side of the car, I open the door for her. I take

her hand, and we walk to the entrance. I start

telling her historical facts I have discovered

over the years, including something I've

heard about. There was supposedly a murder

that took place here a long time ago. I'm still

not sure how much of that was actually true,

but it makes for an interesting tidbit.

Honestly the only thing I know about this

place is the fact that weird things happened

and apparently, I'm mixed up in it. I guess

now Adilyne is unknowingly mixed in it too.

"How is everything so clean and tidy?

Wouldn't everything be dusty and worn

after that long?" she asks as we enter the foyer. She has a point. This place is in immaculate shape for only one old man taking care of it on his own. There must've been someone else here with him or something.

We finally make it to the tower where the library is. As we approach the door, Adilyne admires the symbol decoration on it. She lifts her hand and caresses the Fleur-de-Lis symbol. "This design looks so familiar. I've seen it somewhere before." She continues to tell me that the door seems odd for a castle. Normally they are wooden, but this one is metal. I shrug my shoulders

169

and tell her that maybe they didn't have any wood, or perhaps the owner wanted to be different.

Reaching for the knob, I take a deep breath. "Are you ready?" I ask. She nods in response. As I open the door, I see her face light up and her jaw drop. She looks around and marvels at the shelves of books. Making her way into the room, she approaches the writing desk in the center.

"Wow this is…" she starts before shutting her mouth again. She runs her hands along the binding of the books, stopping to look at a few along the way.

"I thought you might like this room. I

170

discovered it about a year ago when I was

exploring this castle. My family always

drove by it, but I've never been inside until

recently. I've heard so many stories too, I

had to check it out for myself." Most of

what I tell her is true. I just hope I can save

her before she has a chance to really figure

out what that quill can *really* do.

She walks up to the lounge chair under

one of the windows. She sees the design on

the legs that match the door, and I explain I

think that was just the running theme of the

castle. The builders, I'm guessing, were

from Europe, so it would make sense why

that symbol is everywhere.

171

As she walks over to the desk,

something catches my eye out the window. I

walk over and look out at the mountainside.

Getting closer, I realize that is a fucking

dragon. What the hell?! That *has* to be the

other dragon the man wrote about in that

journal. How else would you explain it? I

just hope to God that

Adilyne doesn't see it and freak the hell

out. That's the last thing I want on our date,

for her to freak out or lose it on a day that

is supposed to be a fantastic one.

I'll just have to investigate it more

after I drop her off at home. I'll come back

here and find it and get to the bottom of

what is going on. *If* they want to talk.

"Whose notebook is this?" she asks, flipping through a notebook she must've found on one of the shelves. I don't recognize it. "I'm not sure. It looks like it's been here for a while. If I'd have to guess, it's been here for close to a century," I answer, turning back to the window and keeping an eye on that dragon.

Honestly, I don't even know who these books belonged to. If I had to venture a guess, it would be Elizabeth, the owner's wife. From what I heard, she loved reading and writing. She would sit for hours writing in her journal and gushing about how noble her husband was and describing the things going on around her at the time.

If I could find that journal, I'd destroy it. That journal is the same one the old man used to write curses into existence. Namely, mine and that poor girl who was cursed as a dragon as well.

Chapter Twelve

We made it to her place in record time. I have just over an hour before I have to be at the cave. That gives me plenty of time to say goodnight to Adilyne and make it to the castle.

"I had a great day!" she says as we

stand outside her door. She looks up at me
and I get lost in her beautiful eyes. "I did
too. I hate for it to end, but we have to sleep
sometime," I reply with a smirk. She laughs
and I swear it is the most glorious sound I
have ever heard in my life. I cannot believe
how lucky I am to have found her again.
We've only been dating for a short time, but
I feel like I'm falling hopelessly in love with
her.

I lean in and feel the bolts surge
through me as our lips touch. Grabbing the
back of her head, I deepen the kiss,
exploring her mouth with my tongue. She
tastes like heaven. Grabbing my arms,

Adilyne moans with pleasure. Every time we kiss, I'm entranced by her. Time moves slower and I get lost in her.

I reluctantly pull back and rest my forehead to hers. I wait for my breathing to slow before admitting, "You are so enchanting. I don't think I'll ever get enough of you." I stare at her lips as we stand there for another moment.

Her lips lift in a shy smile as her cheeks turn a delicious rosy color. "Back at ya," she quips. Maybe I'm having the same effect on her as she has had on me.

Leaning in for one last kiss, we say goodnight and she opens the door. "I really had a great day. Thank you," she tells me again. She smiles, leaning her head on the door.

I can't help but grin. "Same. You're very welcome." I grab and kiss the back of her hand before turning and heading back to my car. The night has just begun for me.

The clock ticks by as I stand here in the garden of the castle, waiting for the opportunity to arise to hopefully talk to that other dragon. *I can help. If that is the dragon from the journal, I may need to help deciphering what they say. Of course, if it is the same one, then 'she' may need some help.* Well, 'she' was a dragon during the day. So, if she was indeed cursed and never reversed it, wouldn't that mean that she can shift of her own volition? *I would assume so; however, we will not know until we face her.* We shift and he takes the lead. Taking to the sky, we fly above the trees in search of that dragon. She has to be around here somewhere. *Unless she got tired from flying all day and decided to rest.* If she did, it won't bode well for me. We need to find her. She may hold some answers to questions I've had for so many years now.

We fly over the edge of the city, and still nothing. Dipping down below the tree line, we land and start the search by foot. Luckily, the trees are tall and wide enough for us to easily walk around. *It's been almost an hour. I don't think she's here.*

I'm getting to the point where I just want to go back to Adilyne. I need her comfort and scent around me. I'm sick and tired of looking for people who are so damned hard to find. I swear, if I could only find that

dragon, she could help me in some way. She's lived through the same shit I have.

I feel a presence around. She is here somewhere. We just need to fly and get a better vantage point; my dragon says as we shoot up into the air.

As soon as we're high enough, we see something flying around in the distance. We get closer and, sure enough, there she is. Flying up behind her, we quietly follow her until she swoops down to land. We maintain our distance, still keeping her in sight. Once we land, she turns to face us. Her eyes widen and she stands there staring.

A few minutes pass before her eyes squint, she slowly walks towards us. "Who are you? What are you doing here following me?" she asks in a gravelly yet very female tone. I was right! This *is* the dragon that man turned so long ago.

181

Before we can answer, I shift back into human form. She steps back, nearly tripping on a log. Her eyes narrow to slits.

"I'm Tallon. I have been spending years in search of the man responsible for cursing me to live my nights as a dragon. I have no control over it, and I need more answers." She just stands there staring at me. She stares at me for so long, I start feeling the need to cover myself from her.

Suddenly, she shifts out of her dragon form and walks behind a tree. She comes out from behind it a minute later fully clothed, probably ones she had stored here. She starts towards me, her black hair blowing behind

182

her. She stops in front of me, her brown eyes eyeing me with curiosity. "You're new, aren't you? You haven't quite become one with your dragon yet." It doesn't sound like a question. She must've gone through the process. "Not yet. It's just a matter of days. Wait, are you Scarlet Searles, daughter of Edward Searles?" I question.

She tilts her head to the side, squinting her eyes. "How do you know my name?"

So, she *is* the same one I read about in that journal! I knew it. "While looking for the man who did this to me, I came across his journal and found a section in there that talked about you. How you were diagnosed

183

with Dragonism and found out that was the reason I was cursed."

She crosses her arms across her chest and looks at me up and down. "Obviously, Jetson did not know any better. He's been trying too hard to 'fix' me. I guess he still doesn't get it. I don't need another dragon. The cure for Dragonism is to find a *human* to love you for who you've become. Don't get me wrong, you're good looking, but I just don't feel it. You would be nothing but a toy that I can play with and toss away. I have been in search of human love, but all I've found is heartbreak and players. I guess I am destined to live my long existence alone." She sits on the root of a tree, her knees brought up to her chest. Wait, did she just say long existence? She knows the old man.

I walk up to her and sat across from her. "Wait, are you telling me that even if/when I become one with the dragon inside me, I will live forever until I find a human to love me *and* my dragon?!" That is some heavy shit. Although it would be awesome as hell to potentially live forever, I don't want to. I would lose all the people I love. My mom, Adilyne, the friends I've made along the way. They would go on and live their lives and die when the time comes. I

185

don't want to watch them as I live, and they grow old and die. She nods sadly. "I'm afraid so. That's why I've been around for over a hundred years. I still have yet to find someone. I just hope you have better luck."

"So, you know the man who did this to me?

Jetson?"

She nods. "Yes. He was a father figure to me. He was the gardener of the castle, but to me he was much more than that. While my father was off on trips or dealing with business, Jetson was there for me. He took me on walks around the rose garden and showed me all of the secret areas of the castle. I adored him. But then he became obsessed when we found out I contracted Dragonism. No one knows how; to this day I still don't know. One evening I just started to turn, and Jetson became frantic. He had a cousin who was a scientist that tested my blood for any cause, and they found nothing. He's been obsessed ever since. He thought he had found the cause about twenty-five years ago, but he was wrong."

That's a lot of information for one evening. I am exhausted. I need to figure out how I'm going to proceed. "One more question before I go…" She stands and shrugs. "Sure." "Does your dragon talk to you?" She laughs, nodding her head. "She sure does. She's also a big pain in my ass." I laugh too. I know all too well.

We make plans to meet later so she could try her best to help me as best as she can. I just need to find out how I'm going to get that quill away from Adilyne without hurting her.

I sit in the office, staring at page after page of companies' SEOs. All that's going on in my mind is Adilyne. I *need* to see her, to make sure she's okay. The longer

she has that quill, the higher the risk of her

getting hurt. I look up at the clock. *Good,*

it's lunch time. I'll go pay Adilyne a visit.

Walking into the Castlewide Media

building, I realize why Adilyne is so

enamored with this place. It has a sort of

welcoming feel to it. "Good afternoon, sir.

How can I help you?" a young woman asks

from behind the counter to my right. "I'm

looking for Adilyne Grace," I politely reply.

She smiles and walks out from around the

counter. "Of course! I'll take you to her.

Does she know you're coming?" "No, it's a

surprise."

189

Leading me around a corner, she points to where Adilyne sits at her desk. "Thank you," I say as I make my way to her and stand behind her chair. She stretches, bringing her arms in front of her. I smirk as she starts to push her chair back, bumping into me. "What the…" she says, turning her head.

"Hey, beautiful. We've got to stop meeting like this." I try my damnedest to keep a straight face and fail. She jumps up and wraps me in a hug. "What are you doing here? Don't you have a job?" she asks, fumbling and covers her mouth. "Shit… Wait I didn't mean to imply…" I grab her head in my hands and bring her head to my

chest. I kiss her on the forehead and breathe

in that delicious scent. As I laugh slightly,

she looks up at me. "Well…I'm on my lunch

break and decided to take you out to lunch

where we first 'met.'" I can't help but smile

at the last word.

She smiles, and after telling her boss

she was going out to lunch, we headed for

the door. We sit down by the window. "It's

kinda funny how we met here," she says.

I reach over, grabbing her hands and

holding them in mine. A chuckle escapes

me. "That's how the best stories are told,

aren't they? 'It all started when they bumped

191

into each other…" It feels like so long ago, meeting here. In reality it's only been a few months. We both laugh. When I'm with her all the troubles surrounding my life.

After putting in our order, we sit there staring at each other. She has everything I need. Beauty, brains, and humor. I still don't know how I got so lucky. I look out the window. How could I get that quill away from her without hurting her. *Couldn't I just tell her the truth and let her come to the decision on her own? Why do I have to take it from her? If you're right and she is 'the one', then why can't I just be honest with her.* The dragon seems to be too quiet today. It's

192

getting on my fucking nerves. I readjust my sleeves. The last thing I need is someone seeing the scales and think I'm some monster

Adilyne looks up from her drink "So... I read more of that journal I found at the castle." When I raise my eyebrow at her, she continues. "It's getting really interesting. So far, Edward went missing, and the author had seen some sort of creature in their garden. I think something happened to them and whatever 'creature' she was talking about may have killed them or something..."

Oh, dear God. She has the journal too. Shit. And she's fucking reading it. It's only a matter of time before she gets to the part where I am involved. I'm not ready yet. I need more time. I shake my head. "That's not a good idea. I don't think you should read any more. In fact, you should probably return it to where you found it…" She interrupts, questioning me as I knew she would, but I can only tell her so much. She rips her hands out of mine. As she begins to argue with me, her cheeks tinge red with frustration. I have to diffuse the situation.

"Just please take it back. I don't have a really good feeling about it. If what you're saying about what happened, then whosever journal that is may come back and do God knows what to you. I have a sick feeling in the pit of my stomach when it comes to that journal. Please, I don't want anything to happen to you. Maybe you should give it to me. I'll make sure it's put back where it belongs." I try my best to sound as sincere as I can. It takes tremendous effort not to panic at the moment.

She looks at me incredulously. "I will make sure to not read any more of it. I understand, but you have to trust me. There is no reason for you not to trust me. You need to have more faith in me. I promise. I *will* take it back."

I apologize to her and explain that it's not that I don't trust her. I'm just worried. Although most of what I tell her about that

195

book is true. I can't get myself to tell her everything yet.

After her promise to return it and not to read any more of it, our lunch comes and we eat. She seems to relax, and my heart starts beating at a normal pace. We talk about anything and everything other than that journal. I swear that book and quill will be the death of me one day. I just have to make sure she lives up to her promise to return it, then all I have to do is get rid of that quill. After those are out of the way, we can finally live a relatively normal life.

Chapter Thirteen

"I'm going to use the bathroom; I'll be right back." Adilyne makes her way to the restrooms.

Looking at where she was sitting, I notice her purse. How did I not know she had the journal? *Maybe the quill is with her,*

197

I try again with my dragon. I haven't heard
from him all day.

You should check before she gets back.
This would be the prime opportunity to do it.
This chance may not come back again, he
finally speaks up. *It's about time you make*
an appearance. I feel him roll his eyes.

I look back towards the restroom to
make sure the coast is clear, then go for it. If
my mom saw me now, she would flip her
lid. She raised me better, but desperate times
call for desperate measures.

Quickly digging into her bag, I find an
old worn cloth. Unwrapping it, I find the
quill and a bottle of ink wrapped inside. I

rewrap it and slip it into my pocket and arrange her bag exactly how she left it. One problem down; now I just need to get that journal, and everything will be as it should. Perhaps one day she will forgive me.

"I'd love to sit here all day with you…" she says as she suddenly gets back to the table, "…but I really need to get back to work before I'm late." I stand and pull her into a hug, kissing the top of her head. *I hope you know Adilyne that I love you with everything I am. I'm so sorry for doing this, but it's for your protection. I would die if anything happened to you.* I wish I could tell her all that, but I can't. The words don't

come. We walk out hand in hand. I kiss her and
we part ways. I just hope she will forgive me,
and we can pick up where we left off. For now, I
need to find a place for the quill that no one will
ever find discover. All that's left to do now is
get the journal.

Standing outside her apartment. I try
hard to steel myself for what I'm about to
do. It's tearing me up inside, but it has to be
done.

Taking a deep staggered breath, I
reach for the doorknob. It's unlocked. Relief

and annoyance course through me. Why would she leave her door unlocked for just anyone to enter? Does she have that much trust in her neighbors?

I look around and as luck would have it, I find the journal on her desk. *Thank God, I don't have to take too long to look for it. She has it in plain sight.*

Great, now let's go before she returns and finds you here, my dragon says. I agree; there's no time to waste. Grabbing the journal, I make my way out. There's still so much for me to do.

The drive to my house feels like a long one. The weight of what I just did lies heavily on my shoulders. I fight the urge to turn around and tell Adilyne everything, wondering if perhaps she'll understand. But reality kicks in and knocks me upside the head. How can she? She'd think I'm crazy.

Pulling into my driveway, I rush to the front door. I need to get this stuff far away from here. I walk through the door, and suddenly I start feeling a strange sense wash over me. *What's happening?* I ask the only other one that can help. *It is starting. The time has come. Within the next hour, we will become as one.*

Suddenly I feel a strange tingling sensation under my shirt. Rolling the sleeves back, I watch as scales fall out. *Once all the scales have fallen, the process will be complete.* Shit, all this has happened so fast. I guess the decision's been made for me. I suppose it's not *all* bad. I won't have to

work around a certain time of night
anymore.

A noise in the back yard captures my
attention. I squint my eyes and widen in
surprise. "How did you know where I live?"
I ask Scarlet as she changes into her human
form. She picks up a bag, which I'm
assuming her dragon carried, takes clothes
out of it and dresses. "I simply followed you
the other night when you left. I was curious
as to where you resided." She walks to the
patio and sits at the table. "Furthermore, I
have to tell you one more thing. That girl
you've been seeing has a gift of sorts. It
goes beyond the quill and the 'magic' the

quill possesses. Although Jetson makes his own magic stories with it, the quill is very particular about who it 'allows' to wield it."

I stare at her, my eyebrows knitting together. I squint my eyes at her. "How long have you been following me and how would you know about Adilyne?" Scarlet laughs, crosses her arms and leans back in the chair. "I have no other place to go. I've been around for over a hundred years. I'm stuck here. For a long time, I had Jetson. I would keep an eye on him, except for that unfortunate day in the park. I was falling for a man who turned out to be a royal pain in the ass. But I digress. I've had my eyes on you. I guess I wanted to look after you in a way and make sure you don't cause or run into any trouble. It wasn't until I saw Adilyne pick up the quill Jetson 'dropped' when I realized fate has stepped in."

Sitting in the chair opposite her, I contemplate all she just told me. She's been around all along and is just now making herself known? "That's a lot to take in at once…" All words escape me for the moment. So many questions pop in my head, yet words don't seem to form. That's a first for me. I've always known what to say, but not now.

"So, from what I understand, you now

have the quill and journal. I don't believe

that is a good decision to take it from her.

The quill chose her, and it *will* find its way

back to her. Believe me, I made that mistake

once trying to get it away from Jetson, but no

matter what I did, he always seemed to have

it back." I shake my head. "I have to try. I

don't want it to destroy her or worse. I have

to do something. What if you're wrong and

it was just a freak accident that she

happened across it?" Standing up, I realize

more scales have fallen. I take a mental

count of how many are left. Only about

three remain.

"Not long now. The process has already

begun for you…" she starts. I don't hear much after that. I walk towards the middle of the yard, feeling the need to fly. "I only have…" Two more scales fall. "Correction, about one more scale before the process has completed, according to my dragon. All I know is that I need to get this quill and all of the curses that come with it as far away from Adilyne as possible," I insist. She shakes her head as she stands and walks my way. "You still don't get it. That quill *will* make its way back to her, whether you like it or not. Inevitably, it's up to her whether *she* wants to accept the power or not." I'm not going to listen to any more of this. I need to protect her at all costs. I didn't go this far to fail

208

now. I don't even really know this woman, how am I supposed to know she's telling me the truth? I feel the last scale falling, leaving one last scar.

Suddenly I feel as the power courses through me, new and foreign. It's an exhilarating feeling. I look up and around me. Things look and smell different. They feel different too. "Oh, I know that look all too well. That's how I felt the first time as well. The air smells crisper, the colors look more vibrant, and the feeling of the air around you feels like you've been wrapped in a great blanket of sunshine, florals and cool afternoon air." Scarlet leans against a tree, smiling at me. The need to fly and be free gets stronger with each passing minute.

Try it. You can now shift on your own, all you have to do is call to me and I will surface. I do as I'm told. Shifting this time is not so painful; in fact, all the pain of shifting that I had before is nonexistent. I feel free. Looking down, I realize my clothes have been torn to shreds and the quill is laying there still wrapped in the cloth. *How do we shift back,* I ask, not sure of anything at the moment. *I simply do what you did and call you to the surface. It's a fairly easy process. We will get the hang of it in no time.*

Shifting back, I grab the quill. I need to

get a bag to carry with me at all times. Scarlet managed to carry one in her talons, perhaps I can do the same.

Running back outside, bag in hand, I ready myself. Looking around, I don't see Scarlet. She must've left. Well, at least I don't have to worry about her being at my house for now.

I shift and take to the sky. Flying around the massive backyard, I notice a figure standing just on the other side of the shrubs. We fly closer and I'm shocked. It's Adilyne! *What's she doing here?* I ask, knowing full well my dragon knows as much as I do. *You* did *take the quill and*

211

journal from her. She's smart; she most likely figured it all out and came here to confront you. We fly away as fast as we can towards the cave. I need to bury this quill as far under as I can get. Having dragon claws really helps in situations like this. It makes digging faster and farther than any human can go. With the quill safely hidden away, I can start to breathe better, knowing Adilyne will be safe.

When I turn to leave, I almost crash into Scarlet. "What the fuck?! Why are you following me?" I shout. We both shift back to human form. "You *do* know that quill will not stay in that cave for long," Scarlet urges.

"Like I told you, it is meant for Adilyne and it will find its way back to her." Rolling my eyes, I make my way to the front of the cave. "Even if that happens, I'll make damn sure she doesn't get hurt because of it." Shifting back to dragon form, we take to the sky.

Chapter Fourteen

Adilyne

One Month Later...

"I can't believe that just happened!" Melinda screams as we stand there in shock. We had been staring at the dragon for I don't know how long, laying seemingly lifeless at our feet. I'm still racking my brain around what just happened.

"That wasn't what I intended to do, Mel!" I reply, gesturing to the creature. "It was supposed to be a lizard, not a frickin' dragon!" I pick up my bag off the ground and toss the quill and notebook in. I glance at the creature one last time, unsettled by the sight.

Did that seriously just happen? How could everything have gone so wrong? All the other times I had used the quill, everything went according to plan, so why was this time so different?

Mel grabs my hand and brings me back to the present. "It's ok, Addi. It's over

215

now. I know you didn't mean for any of this to happen." She lets go of my hand and stands in front of me, grabbing me by the shoulders. "Listen, it's dead now. We don't have to worry about it, okay? Let's just get out of here, and we'll come back tomorrow and figure out what to do with it. It's not like it's going anywhere," she snickers. I answer with a nod, glancing at the creature one last time, and start out of the cave to head home.

After finding out Tallon was actually a freaking dragon, Mel and I freaked out at first, then went back to my house. The whole situation was crazy; we just needed time to process what had just happened.

Once we got back to my house, I noticed something sitting on my desk. When I got closer, I was surprised to find a familiar old cloth wrapped object. Mel and I looked at each other in confusion. We had searched this whole apartment top to bottom, and it was nowhere to be found, so how did it get here? Of course, lately it shouldn't surprise me that it appeared. That's how things happen around this object.

Unwrapping it to make sure it *was* what I had thought it was, I found I was correct. I could've sworn I looked everywhere, but maybe not.

Tonight, after we get through the woods, we part ways. I arrive home, struggling to dig the keys out of my bag. I swear, I don't know why I carry so much crap in this stupid thing. It always takes me forever to find anything.

After a few minutes, I finally find them and walk through the door. Wow, that was the most stressful thing I think I've ever encountered in my entire life. The only thing that even comes remotely close was a few months ago. I can't even go there right now.

A burning sensation creeps into my eyes. I rub them, hoping to bring some relief.

It doesn't. I think the only thing that would help is to get some long-needed sleep.

I lie in my bed, stare at the ceiling, and think about what happened today. I shouldn't have let Mel talk me into creating that ridiculous story. What was I thinking? Of course, little did I know it was going to turn out the way it had. After what feels like an eternity, I start drifting to sleep...

Thick, forest green grass tickles my ankles, and giant weeping willows sway before me. I swing around, my brows knit to a v. The willows surround me, towering over my head.

An orange sky glows through the small spaces between the willows. It must be

219

getting late. I look down at my feet, feeling

the soft brush of the grass

between my toes. Why am I barefoot? I don't

remember going to the woods, let alone

without my shoes.

My surroundings look an awful lot

like the woods I was just in with Mel and

that Dragon. I start to make my way down

the dirt path to my right, hoping to find

whatever it is that brought me here. My feet

are throbbing from what feels like two miles

of walking, and I stop. Ahead of me I see

something through the trees. Whatever it is,

seems to be alive... and huge.

As I get closer, something lets out a

low grumble, and my heart bangs in my chest. A sense of dread washes over me.

The creature steps out from the willows. It must be at least ten feet tall. It breaks off a branch and scratches its back, its dry scales sloughing off in patches. Suddenly it turns its head in my direction, and its gaze falls on mine. I freeze, caught in its spell. What was I thinking?! It's unnerving standing in front of this creature, not knowing what it's thinking or even planning. I do, however, feel a sense of calm as I look this creature in the eye. Something about it seems so gentle. I make my way closer to it.

As if out of nowhere, it charges at me. I

turn and run in the direction I came. I have no idea what good that will do since the creature is much bigger than me and can catch me in an instant, but hey it's worth a shot, right?

I halt at the edge of a cliff. The creature's hot breath flows around me like the wind on a breezy afternoon. I swing around, and I am face to face with it. It opens its mouth, and I scream...

I shoot up in my bed. What in the world was that about? I look around my room, my brows furrowing. The dream fades. I shake my head and glance at the clock on my

222

nightstand. Ugh, it's too early. I guess I'd better get up. There's no point in trying to go back to sleep now. I throw my legs off the bed and stand. I lose my balance for a second, but quickly recover before I fall flat on my face. I make my way to the bathroom.

I stare at my reflection in the mirror, my unruly crimson hair sticking out in odd places. I blow a strand from my eyes and throw the whole thing into a messy bun. I need to go to the cave today and check on that dragon. What should I do about it? I hope somehow it just dissolves into thin air and takes care of itself. That would make my job so much easier. I guess I could call Mel

223

and have her meet me; I could use the help.
We *could* dig a huge hole in the far back of
the cave and bury it. It's not like anyone
ever goes into that cave anyway. It's highly
unlikely it will ever be discovered.

As I finish getting ready, bits and
pieces of my dream come into view. It was
about some sort of creature. Was that dream
a glimpse into the future? Telling me what is
to come? Lord, I hope not. What if the
dragon isn't there? What if we were wrong,
and it wasn't dead? That would be a
disaster! I grab my bag, digging for my
phone as I head out the door.

"Hey, Mel," I greet as she answers the

phone. "I'm heading out to the cave, wanna meet me there?"

"I'm so sorry, I can't today. Something came up. I can meet you tomorrow and figure out what to do from there."

"That's alright. I'll just head out there anyway. I need to make sure it's still there. I have this feeling in my gut something is off."

"I'm sure it's still there. Be careful though. The woods can be dangerous all alone. Keep me updated on everything." After we say our goodbyes, I hop in my car, praying along the way that it's still there.

I arrive at Hollow Point in less than five minutes. It's not that far of a walk from my house to the cave but I needed the car for other things I need to do today, so it just made sense to bring it.

As I reach the cave, an overwhelming sense of dread comes over me. I make my way into the cave, afraid of what I might or might not find. I cross my fingers along the way, hoping it was still there, and we didn't just assume it was dead. I reach the place where we left the dragon, and I freeze.

My eyes widen as I stare at the

226

ground. WHAT IN THE WORLD??!! The dragon is GONE! I grab the sides of my head, digging my fingers into my hair as I pace back and forth. Where could it be? It was lying lifeless here last night. The only thing I can think of is that it wasn't dead, and it's out there somewhere.

Wait a minute... what if it's further towards the back of the cave? It *was* late, and I was driven to the point of exhaustion. Maybe I'm just in the wrong spot. I jog to the back of the cave. Please let it be there, please let it be there, I chant as I go. I stop in my tracks and drop to my knees, running my fingers through my hair. I look all around me at the dirt.

J.L. Hinds

IT'S GONE!! WHAT AM I

GOING TO DO NOW??!!

Tallon

I can't believe Adilyne did that! Luckily for Scarlet, she cannot die by the hands of the quill. Of course, in Adilyne's defense, it *did* look like Scarlet was after her.

Scarlet should have gone about it differently instead of scaring the bejesus out of Adilyne and Melinda. Little did I know Adilyne would know how to wield the quill in order to 'save their lives'.

Sitting here anxiously waiting for Scarlet is the most nerve-wracking thing. Although every fiber of my being wants to run to Adilyne, I stop myself. She still needs to digest everything that happened. She may have thought that was me, and I don't think I can face her until I figure things out. What if she gets the quill and does something she may regret? I would not be able to live with myself knowing I did that to her.

Scarlet flies in and shifts upon landing. She quickly dresses and sits down beside me. "You know, you could've gone about that differently," I tell her, my brows furrowing. She shrugs. "Well, can't change what's already been done." She cups the back of her neck and rolls her head. "Damn, her power is pretty strong though. For a second, I thought she was actually going to really kill me."

I shake my head and chuckle. "Yeah, you got lucky. Little did we know she was going to use the magic to try and kill you."

"I knew the power of it. Like you said, I should have approached her differently. I don't know exactly what she intended to do or what she wrote, but it felt like I got hit by

231

a thousand heavy boulders. That is what

knocked me out, and almost killed me."

Crossing my arms in front of me, I stare

out into the yard. "I don't know how to

explain to her why I did what I did." She

draws my attention to her. "Just go to her.

Tell her everything." She leans in. "I

recommend doing it as yourself though.

There's no telling what she would do to

you." I stand and go inside, and Scarlet

follows me. "Perhaps you're right. I'll go

talk to her," I reply as I walk to the front

door, readying myself to leave. She huffs as

she stands beside me at the door. "I didn't

say to do it now. Not after all that happened

232

today."

Waving her out the door, I follow and lock it behind me. "I want to do it sooner rather than later. I know with everything going on, she may throw me out or slam the door in my face, but I'll lose my mind if I don't explain to her why I did what I did. I'll see you when I see you. I'm glad you're okay." We part ways as I make my way to Adilyne.

Standing outside her apartment, I look up and see her in the bathroom, dressed and looks like she's ready to go to bed. I guess it's now or never.

Walking up to her apartment, I think hard about what to say. I just need to get it all off my chest. If she slams the door in my face, I will accept it. I need to be honest with her. Obviously what Scarlet told me about the quill was true. Adilyne had received it back and seemed to know how to wield it. I hate it but I *have* to put more trust in her if she accepts who I really am now.

I knock and wait for her to answer. It feels like an eternity passed before she opens

234

the door. She stands there, hair in a perfectly

messy bun. Her eyes widen we she sees me.

"Tallon? What are you doing here?" she

asks leaving the door cracked and placing

her hands on her hips. I don't blame her one

bit. Seems like she's handling it better than I

probably would if I was in her position.

"Can I please come in? We need to

talk. I have a lot to tell you." My voice is

full of sincerity. Looking me up and down,

she takes a deep breath, opens the door more

and lets me in.

I follow her to the living room and sit

on the couch, facing her as she sits on the

opposite end, crossing her arms. "What can

235

you possibly say? You lied to me. I feel like
I don't even know you. Was anything you
told me about yourself true? Are you really
from Windham?" She bombards me with
questions.

"Everything I told you was true. The
only thing I didn't tell you was what I am
and how I got to be that way." Taking a deep
breath, I let it all out. I tell her everything.
How the quill was used to curse me as a
baby and all I have learned along the way.
She sits there, tears welling up in her eyes.
The last thing I wanted was for her to pity
me. "I've learned to live with it. The only
thing that scared me lately was lying to you

and hurting you. I felt like I had no control over anything, and it was driving me crazy." I pause, watching her reaction. She stands up and places her hands on her hips. "You have that little trust and faith in me?" She sounds hurt. She walks closer to me, her eyes flaming in frustration. "I know a little about crazy. From the moment that quill fell at my feet, it has been one thing after another. I thought I was losing my mind. Then I met you and although strange things still happened, I knew I had someone to keep me grounded. I felt like I was crazy when I thought I saw scales or something similar under your shirt. Then I saw a dragon, which now I assume was you, flying

237

in the distance. It was one thing after another. But with you around, I felt loved and safe. You should've trusted me better to accept what and who you are…"

I couldn't believe what I was hearing. How could she be real? Not only is she being cool about what has happened, but she would've accepted me for what I was? I don't deserve her.

Standing up, I reach for her. She hesitates at first, but then wraps her arms around me. "I'm so sorry," I exhale, "I was stupid and afraid." Taking a deep breath, I pull her back and look at her. She looks up, confused. "I have something else to tell you.

It's going to sound crazy, but I think we've both established that none of this sounds sane…" We both laugh and she nods her head. "Yeah, the crazy ship has already sailed. Whatever you have to say, I'll try my best to keep an open mind."

Walking over to the couch, I have her sit next to me and I face her. Taking a deep breath, I ready myself. *Don't worry, she will be fine. We will be fine. Like I have told you in the past and she recently told you, she wants to know you and wants complete honesty. She will understand.* Sometimes he can be a pain in the ass, but my dragon has a point. "Okay, so you know who and what I am, there's more." She nods, waiting quietly for me to continue. "The dragon side of me talks to me and has told me, since the day I met you, to trust you with our secret. I didn't believe him. All that was on my mind at the time was to find that quill and destroy it, so it doesn't hurt anyone else like it did me. I was cursed by it, and for the longest time, I thought it would never end." Tears stain her cheeks. I pull her into my arms. "I'm okay now, but I was afraid. I am so sorry I put you through all that. I wish I could take it all back and just tell you the truth." Lifting her head and looking into her eyes, I see love and hurt there.

She cups each side of my face. "You are the only one that I have *ever* felt safe around. I understand how hard it was, and how hard it is now, to tell me all this. I love you, Tallon Harcrose, and I know we've only known each other for a short time but I've fallen hard." Her voice is full of vulnerability. "Should you have told me all this from the beginning? Yes, but I *do* understand why. I did about the same thing with that quill. I didn't tell you about it because of everything that has happened. I didn't want you to think I was crazy." She shakes her head and laughs. I love that sound. It warms my heart to hear her laugh. I crave it. I grab the back of her head and kiss

241

her.

Wrapping her arms around my neck, she deepens the kiss. All these years, since my eighteenth birthday, I thought I was cursed. It turns out I was wrong. It all led me to Adilyne. She has been amazing. I can be myself around her. I haven't felt this kind of love, ever.

She sits on my lap. I break the kiss long enough to remove my shirt. She looks down at my chest, rubbing the scars. I lift her head and look her in the eyes. Tears start running down her cheeks and I wipe them away. "What are those scars from? The scales?" she asks hesitantly.

I nod. "They started appearing when I turned eighteen. They hurt at first, but after a while it just felt like tingles. They only started falling off recently. That's a story for another time." She leans in and kisses me. I kiss her back, deepening the kiss.

We lay on the couch after the best evening. Adilyne lifts her head and rests her chin on my bare chest. She is so sexy even with post-coitus hair.

She traces one of my scars with her

243

finger. "What does it mean now that the scales fell off? Do you still have that dragon inside of you?" she asks as she bites her bottom lip.

I smile at her. "Well, he's more a part of me now. I found out recently that, after a period of time, the dragon inside of me and I became one, meaning that I can now choose when and where to shift instead of being forced to shift at a certain time of the night." She smiles and her brows knit to a *v*. I lift her face to mine. "Penny for your thoughts?" I give her my best grin. She shakes her head. "It's a stupid idea that popped into my head…" She shuts her mouth, shaking her head again and laughing.

I laugh with her. "Let me be the judge of that. What is it? Please tell me." I resort to begging but I need her to tell me. The curiosity is now driving me crazy. "I was just thinking about how it must feel to fly. I was also thinking about flying with you." She bites her lip again and it makes me want to have my way with her again. A chuckle escapes my mouth. That's an interesting idea. I've never thought about taking anyone flying. *Is that possible? Will we be able to carry someone when we fly?* I ask the only one that would have the answer. *Of course. She would have to hold on very tight.*

Otherwise, it'll be a horrific death. I roll my eyes. Why does he always have to go there? Adilyne groans. "I told you it was a stupid idea." She buries her face in my chest.

I pick her head up and make her look at me. "I wasn't laughing at you. My dragon was just being an ass and thinking the worst. If we were to take you flying, you would have to hold on tight. I doubt very seriously that there's a harness big enough to fit my dragon." She lifts herself up, crossing her arms and putting her head on top of them "I think I may be able to handle that. We're just going to have to try it first, before leaving the ground." Her smile is infectious.

I can't help but smile. Pulling her up, I kiss her. I have no idea what I did to deserve this woman. Not only has she forgiven me, but she has accepted *all* of me with open arms.

"I love you more than you will ever know, Adilyne Grace. You are amazing," I say against her lips. She deepens the kiss. We spent the rest of the night in each other's arms.

Chapter Sixteen

Waking up with Adilyne curled around me is the best feeling in the world. She looks so peaceful when she sleeps. For once, I'm not waking to dread of what's to come. All I feel with her next to me is hope. Hope for a better future with her in it. The

248

only one besides my mother that loves me for who I have become and who I am. How did I get so lucky?

She moves, unwrapping herself from me and turns, still asleep. I look at the clock. It's still early. I should make breakfast for her. It's the least I can do. Quietly getting out of bed, I slip my pants on and make my way to the kitchen. Digging around, I find what I need and get started.

"What's this?" Adilyne asks as she walks into the kitchen. I turn to see her leaning on the bar. I smile at her. She looks so damn sexy in my t-shirt. It hugs her in all the right places. I swear it looks better on her.

I set the plate in front of her. "I made breakfast," I reply simply. Walking around the bar, I kiss her and push the fallen hair behind her ear. She blushes. I caress her rosy cheek with my thumb. "Now sit and enjoy."

I wink at her and give her my best smirk. I kiss her head and get my plate and sit next to her. "How would you like to go to my place and we can figure out a way to fly with you on my back? It may take some time but I believe we can do it." She almost chokes on her food. I pat her on the back.

"Are you okay?" I ask, laughing yet

concerned.

She holds her chest and takes a drink of

her coffee. She clears her throat. "Yes, I'm

fine. I didn't think you were *actually* going

to take me up on that idea."

"We don't have to do it if you don't

want to. I just thought since you brought it

up and seemed excited at the thought that I'd

give you what you wanted. That's all I want

to do is to make you happy like you've done

for me."

It takes all I have to not fall back when

she throws herself at me, wrapping her arms

251

around my neck. "You make me happy no matter what you do. You don't have to go out of your way for me at any cost. But I appreciate it. I'll get changed." She kisses me and I deepen the kiss. Standing up, I pick her up, our lips still locked together, and I walk to her bedroom.

Opening her front door, I nearly run into a woman with black hair, raising her hand like she was fixing to knock. She jumps back. Then eyes me. "What the hell are you doing here?"

I step back as she walks in. "Mel! What a surprise," Adilyne says, getting between me and Mel. Mel doesn't take her eyes off me, narrowing her gaze and giving me a look that could kill. Did she know what happened? "What are you doing here?" Adilyne asks her as she waves her in. I step aside.

Mel sits on the couch and finally looks at her. "I just wanted to check on you and see how you were

doing. I know this past week has been hard on you." She looks pointedly at me. Adilyne looks at me with an apologetic expression, biting the corner of her lip. "Everything is good. Tallon came by last night and we talked." She waves me over and I stand next to her. She puts her arm around my waist, and I do the same. "We worked it all out and I couldn't be happier."

Mel seems to thaw and stands in front of us, crossing her arms in front of her chest. She eyes me warily then steps in front of me, pointing a finger at me. "You better do right by her. She's been hurt too many times. Dragon or not, I will find a way to end you if harm comes to her." A laugh escapes my chest. I clear my throat when I see the look on her face. "Got it. I promise I will protect her with my life. I feel the same way. I would rather die than let anything happen to her. I thought I was protecting her, but I've learned that it's better to be honest." She nods her head, smiling at Adilyne. She reaches for her and they hug. "I'm so happy for you. After all the shit you've been through, you deserve to be happy."

Adilyne smiles between her and me. "So, are we done now? Everyone happy? I *can* run my own life you know." I laugh and wrap my arms around her kissing her. "We know, we both care for you and want to protect you." Mel clears her throat. "Well, it looks like I interrupted something, so I'll go on my way." She makes her way to the door. She turns to me. "By the way. You're really a frigging dragon?" She looks me up and down, then winks at Adilyne. "Nice." She smiles and leaves. Adilyne laughs and shakes her head. "That woman is a mess." I kiss the top of her head. "You ready?" She nods. "As ready as I can be." I take her hand and we head out to my house.

Chapter Seventeen

"Okay, let's try this again. You almost had it." We've been at it all afternoon. Adilyne was so close this last attempt to stay on my back. "Wait, I have an idea. Do you have any kind of rope?" she asks, chewing on her bottom lip.

I shift back to my human form and put my hands on my hips. "Why?" I don't think I like where this is going.

She laughs and wraps her arms around me and looks up at me. "Don't worry, it's not bad. At least, I don't think so." She looks down as she says the last part. I lift her head up and look in her eyes. "Tell me what you're thinking, please."

She takes a deep breath and walks out of my hold. "You know how there are leads for dogs?" My eyes widen. Oh, I see where she's going with this. "So, you want to put a leash on me?" She laughs and it makes me want to do anything to hear that

258

sound again. I smile. She moves her head side to side and smirks. "Kinda… Fasten it in a way for me to have something to hang onto. Or…" She pauses. "What if I were to write about finding a dragon sized harness."

I feel all the blood rush from my face. No, she cannot use that object. There's no telling what could happen. She rushes over to me and cups my face, looking me in the eyes. I wrap my arms around her instinctively. "Nothing is going to happen. I've written two stories with it, and nothing has happened. I'm not like whoever did this to you. I would *never* do that to anyone. I promise." She takes a sharp intake of breath when she realizes I won't change my mind.

259

"Okay, if it worries you that bad, I won't write with it."

I let go the breath I was holding and shake my head. Closing my eyes, I put my forehead on hers. "It's too soon. I trust you with every fiber of my being, but too much has happened with that quill." She nods and looks into my eyes. "I get it. So… Should we get the rope?" We both laugh. "That sounds like a better plan. I have some in the shed."

After a dozen more tries, I feel confident in Adilyne. "I'd say you're ready."

Her smile grows, then a look of uncertainty crosses her face. "Don't tell me that after all this time, you're having second thoughts." I lift her chin and kiss her.

She melts into my arms and deepens the kiss. She grabs the back of my head and plays with my hair. "Not really. It's just that now I'm getting a little nervous. The only time I've been up in the air, I was surrounded by walls either in a plane or helicopter. I won't have that on your back."

I hold her tighter. "I would never let you fall. Do you trust me?" She nods. "Then trust that I would never let any harm come to you. I am right here." She nods and smiles.

"That's my girl." I kiss her passionately, bringing my forehead to hers. "Let's soar."

"Oh…my…Goodness!!" Adilyne yells. We started out low and slow to break her into it. After about an hour, she wanted to go higher, until we were so high we were flying above the mountains. My favorite place to be. The sound of her joy courses through me. I'm so glad we could do that for her. "Hang on," we tell her as we swoop down for a landing. I feel when she grabs a hold of the scales on our shoulder blades. "I'm ready!" she yells over the wind rushing past.

As we land, my dragon holds his wing out as she uses it as a slide. Once she's safely on the ground, I shift back. She throws her arms around my neck. "That was so much fun. It was so nice to get away from everything." I smile fondly at her. "Now you know how I feel every time we fly."

She tilts her head. "*We*, as in you and your dragon?" she asks, giving me a crooked smile.

"Yes, I consider him a part of me in that when *we* are flying, I am there with him." Scooping her up in my arms, I bring her inside.

"If that wasn't you at the cave, then who was it? Is there another dragon out there?" Adilyne leans on her elbows next to me on the bed, laying on her stomach. I should've known that was going to come up sooner or later. I was just hoping it would be later. I could tell there was a flood of questions waiting to be asked.

Rolling over on my side, I face her, resting my head on my hand. "That was Scarlet Searles. She was going to introduce herself, but she went about it all wrong. I only met her recently. Before you ask, no I've never been with her, and no there are

264

not any more dragons that I know of. She

was the original dragon. She has been

around since 1905."

She sits up in the bed. Her eyes widen.

"Really? How is she still alive? She must be

well over a hundred years old." Her shock

was practically the same response I had

when I came across Scarlet. I didn't know

what to think about it.

"Apparently, back then she had gotten

ill with a sickness they called Dragonism.

That's when you start growing scales and

transition into becoming a dragon. Evidently

the old man she knew, Jetson, heard that in

order for the sickness to be cured, she had to

265

find another dragon that would mate, and they would fall in love, ending Dragonism." I curved my lips into a thin line. Adilyne covers her mouth and gasps. "That's why he cursed you? So, you could be with Scarlet to cure her sickness?"

Slowly, I nod. "However, Scarlet learned along the way that was not the case. She learned that she had to find someone to love her for who she really is dragon and all for her to live a normal life. She hasn't found that yet, so she lives on until she does."

I wipe at the tears flowing down her cheeks and pull her close to me. "I don't understand why she hasn't met anyone yet. That's so sad," Adilyne sniffles. I love how compassionate she is. How she can show compassion for someone she hasn't even met. I think I see why she was chosen by that quill. She may be the one to actually use it the way it was meant to be used.

She kisses me and rushes off the bed. "I have an idea. I don't want to hear *anything* from you about it. I need to get home." Confused yet intrigued, I get up and follow her lead as we get dressed and head to her house.

Once we pull up to her apartment, I grab her hand in mine. "Can you please let me in on what you have planned so I'm not going in blind?" She smiles sweetly at me as I kiss the back of her hand.

She turns in her seat and cups her hand over my cheek. "You have to promise not to overreact or get upset…" Oh great. I know where this is going. I narrow my eyes. "This has something to do with that quill, doesn't it?" I know that I said the quill had chosen her for a reason, but that doesn't mean I want her to have anything to do with it.

She nods then grabs my hand with

both of hers. "Yes. I want to write about Scarlet finding someone who will love her for who and what she is. I've done it before for Mel, and now she's blissfully happy. I just gave her the opportunity. I only wrote about them meeting, I didn't go into detail."

I couldn't help but laugh. Of course! *That's* why she was chosen. Her compassionate nature, the way she helps others with it and doesn't use it for her own selfish needs. Thinking back, when I read that journal, pretty much all that was written with that quill was a selfish. Jetson cursed me to make himself feel better about what was done to Scarlet. He wanted to be painted as the hero who saved her. Why he

269

chose to keep her Dragonism around is

beyond me. She laughs and looks at me with

her head tilted, confusion written all over

her beautiful face. "What's so funny? That's

not exactly the response I was expecting

from you." I shrug. "I was just marveling at

the level of

compassion you have for others. I think

that's why you were chosen for the quill." I

grab her and bring her to my lap, she

straddles me. "You are the best woman I

know. The world is better with you in it."

She grabs the back of my head and kisses

me. Before it goes where I desperately want

it to go, I reluctantly pull back. "There's

time for that later. Don't you have a

mission?" I smirk. She smiles as I open the

driver's side door, letting her out.

"Bella, I'm home," she calls upon

entering the front door. Her dog runs out

from the bedroom. "I'm so happy you're

back, I missed you." I jump back. What the

hell? A talking dog? Well, that's new.

Adilyne laughs and takes my hand,

bringing me back beside her. An apologetic

look crosses her face. "Sorry, I should've

warned you. She was the product of an

experiment I was doing with the quill," she

whispers. I'm assuming it's to spare

Bella's feelings. "I thought I was going

271

crazy after the first story I wrote with the quill about a talking squirrel then I ran into one at the park. I wanted to see if it was true; turns out I wasn't so crazy."

This time we both laugh. Talking animals. I shake my head, not able to wipe the smile off my face. Well, I guess this is my life now.

Adilyne walks to the desk and stops in her tracks. Then frantically searches for something. My eyes widen when I realize what she was looking for. The Quill. I saw it sitting there yesterday. I know, because I had wondered how she had gotten it back before remembering what Scarlet said about it always returning to the chosen one.

"Bella? Have you seen that quill anywhere?"
Bella's head tilted side to side, before she
jumped on the couch, getting herself
comfortable. "A woman came by and got it.
She told me not to tell anyone then she
laughed. I'm assuming because she thought
it was a ridiculous thought. Then she left."

Adilyne looked at me then back at
Bella, then settled on me. "Why?..." was the
only word that came out of her mouth. I
wrapped my arms around her. "I have no
clue. She couldn't possibly do anything with
it." I racked my brain, trying to think of why
Scarlet Searles would do this. "You *will* get
it back. I promise." Keeping that promise is

273

one thing I plan on doing no matter what it takes. *No one* will get in the way of it. I hold Adilyne in

my arms as I figure out a way to get that quill and stopping Scarlet.

To Be Continued…

The Author:

J.L. Hinds is a lover of all things books.
She began her writing journey through
her love of reading. She loves the
escape books bring and wants to create
them for others. She writes Romance as
well as Paranormal. Shestarted her
journey in California, where she was

born then traveled to Missouri and
finally Georgia, where she met and fell
in love with the love of her life. She
now has a beautiful family whom she
loves to heaven and back again.